Mario Huacuja

In the Name of the Son

TRANSLATED FROM THE SPANISH
BY MARTIN BOYD

Order this book online at www.trafford.com
or email orders@trafford.com

Most Trafford titles are also available at major online book retailers.

Translated from the Spanish by Martin Boyd
Original Title: *En el nombre del hijo*

For information on this work and other works by the author, please contact Diálogos Books
at: info@dialogos.ca or visit the website: www.dialogos.ca

Note for Librarians: A cataloguing record for this book is available from Library
and Archives Canada at www.collectionscanada.ca/amicus/index-e.html

Printed in Victoria, BC, Canada.

ISBN: 978-1-4251-9080-4 (soft)
ISBN: 978-1-4251-9082-8 (ebook)

*We at Trafford believe that it is the responsibility of us all, as both individuals
and corporations, to make choices that are environmentally and socially sound.
You, in turn, are supporting this responsible conduct each time you purchase a
Trafford book, or make use of our publishing services. To find out how you are
helping, please visit www.trafford.com/responsiblepublishing.html*

*Our mission is to efficiently provide the world's finest, most comprehensive
book publishing service, enabling every author to experience success.
To find out how to publish your book, your way, and have it available
worldwide, visit us online at www.trafford.com*

Trafford rev. 8/17/2009

 www.trafford.com

North America & international
toll-free: 1 888 232 4444 (USA & Canada)
phone: 250 383 6864 ♦ fax: 812 355 4082 ♦ email: info@trafford.com

For Lucy, which is the name of my daughter

PART ONE

1

ONE OF THE most striking memories of my early childhood is that of my encounter with the Statue of Liberty. I would have been four or five years old, and the sight of it filled me with awe; I had never seen a woman so big. Everything about her was larger than life. Her green copper color, the strength of her arm reaching into the sky, the elegance of her tunic, the golden flame of her torch and her vacant expression marked me forever.

It seemed as if the world had been orchestrated to bring me to that moment. My mother and I had boarded the ferry at Battery Park after walking around the walls of Clinton Castle, and I had barely begun to rock with the waves in one of the ferry's indoor seats when sleep overtook me. On waking, before I'd completely shaken off my slumber, the Statue loomed over me with all the force of her two hundred and twenty tons, and as my bewildered eyes passed over her figure I couldn't decide whether she was the colossal virgin of a Catholic church or a petrified monster that had escaped from my worst nightmares.

In those years, while I spent my childhood amid electric cars that whirred like pneumatic drills as they crashed into the walls of my bedroom, New York was undergoing a period of formidable expansion. In the neighborhood around Central Park South, the stores on Fifth Avenue were attracting customers from all over the world with their opulent display windows. Park Avenue was enjoying an age of splendor with its stratospherically priced apartments. At the southern end of Manhattan, the Village and Soho had become a magnet for writers, musicians, actors, filmmakers and painters from the rest of the country and from Europe, and not very far from Trinity Church, to the south of Tribeca, they had just finished the Twin Towers of the World Trade Center, which would be the tallest buildings in the world. It was the era when the United States was leading a crusade against communism in Vietnam, and still basking in the glory of having put the first man on the moon. Away up there, on that distant surface of craters and white dust, they had proudly planted the stars and stripes, identical to the ones that hung from the buildings of the Rockefeller Center.

Of course, I had absolutely no idea about any of this, nor was I aware that beneath the nation's façade of invincibility bubbled a tumult of social and racial tensions, which periodically exploded to the surface. Sometimes in the streets I would hear screams, I would see people running, a body on the sidewalk covered with a sheet, but these seemed to me isolated incidents of no importance. My life in those days was quite peaceful, and, on holidays, an endless stream of wondrous discoveries.

That morning, when I saw the rays of Liberty's crown, I imagined she was a goddess, a divinity emerging from the waters and challenging the world with the sheer force of her presence. On the tiny island where she stood was a crowd of people, but there was something in the air that made me feel alone and small before her. "Liberty", muttered the tourists who crowded round the foot of her pedestal to photograph her profile. *"La libertad"* said my mother, as she carried me in one arm and pointed with the other. I listened to her, and opened my eyes wide to take in the colossal dimensions of her stature, and as I did so I hugged my mother's neck tightly to feel the protection of her closeness, because the statue provoked in me a certain sense of profound terror. Perhaps it was then that I learned, directly and definitively, that my mother would always be there to protect me from the deliriums and dangers of liberty.

2

I LIVED WITH my mother in a brownstone building on the Upper East Side of Manhattan, far from the bustle and the glamour of the island's south side, in a part of town omitted from the travel guides. Although the building was not far from Lexington and Park Avenues, its location to the north – it was on 112th Street, next to Jefferson Park – placed it close to the poorest neighborhoods of New York. Nevertheless, as my mother always said, we enjoyed the privilege of living in Manhattan. That made all the difference. We didn't live in Brooklyn, or Queens, or the Bronx, like most Mexicans. We were residents of the Big Apple, the heart of the world, and this fact filled us with pride.

Our neighbors were not exactly members of high society. Mr. Morrison, who lived next door, was a raggedy looking man, with greasy hair permanently plastered to his forehead, a scraggy, reddish beard and a frayed t-shirt with the name of the Yankees scrawled across the front. He was not an unpleasant person; he generally greeted us enthusiastically with a military salute when he saw us. But there was something in his absent stare that made me uneasy. My mother avoided his company, and when she spoke of him to me she said he was a bad sort. It probably didn't help that he was missing a leg, shattered by the shrapnel from a grenade in the killing fields of Southeast Asia. In hindsight, I regard him with a certain pity, but as a child I saw him as strange and dangerous. He was sometimes seized by violent outbursts that drove him to curse loudly and smash objects against the walls. His wife was patient and longsuffering, and when she took him out for a walk in the park in his wheelchair she pinned his war medals to his chest, and sang soft lullabies in his ear as if he were a baby.

Across the hall from our apartment, at the top of the spiral staircase, lived Mrs. Wharton and her two Yorkshire terriers, Wendy and Pimpinela. She was a grey-haired woman advanced in years, whose considerable weight made walking a huge effort for her, and she swayed like a ship at sea as she moved. When she descended the wooden stairs of the apartment building, the banister groaned under the mere weight of her arm, and when she sat on one of the iron benches in Jefferson Park her body took up the space of two people. I remember the time my mother and I met her by chance on the subway at Lexington Station, holding herself up by one of the overhead rails in the middle of the crowd. Suddenly, as often would happen, the train came to an abrupt halt, and Mrs. Wharton's monumental bulk came tumbling down on top of the passengers around her. Several people helped her to her feet, but when the train lurched back into movement she collapsed once again. I found this spectacle hilarious, because I was at the age when I used to enjoy watching *Laurel and Hardy* on TV, and the scene seemed to me something reminiscent of their bumbling misadventures. But as nobody else was laughing, I bit my tongue.

Mrs. Wharton was a dark-skinned woman, but not as dark as the Manleys. They were a family of three children and two parents all born in Jamaica, who lived on the floor below ours. Although the children were all older than I was, and we therefore never became friends, I felt a strong sense of admiration for them. They were a joyful bunch, always laughing with teeth so perfectly white that they made me envious, and constantly slapping rhythmically on any object that came within reach. Whenever they went out together, they always looked as if they were on their way to a parade. They would sing and dance, keeping rhythm with resonant little sticks, and calling out incomprehensible phrases in Jamaican Patois. The racket they made didn't go down well at all with Mr. Morrison, and he would often come out into the hall, his face twisted with rage, to shut them up, but the Manleys seemed immune to his threats. They simply lowered the volume of their chanting until they got to the bottom of the stairs, and when they got out to the street they resumed more spiritedly than before. I would lean out of the window of our apartment that looked over the street to enjoy a little more of their lively caterwauling, and follow them with my eyes until they disappeared from view.

That music-filled joy, shared by the only nuclear family living in our building, was cut short one day by police intervention. One winter's morning, shortly after the first snowfall, several patrol cars pulled up diagonally around the entrance to our building, and after that the father of the Manley family disappeared completely. I never saw him again, and perhaps neither did his children, because from that day their music stopped. They became quiet and solemn, more like me than their former selves.

My bedroom was small, with a window that looked out over the inner yard of the building, and a closet that held not only my clothes, but my old rocking horse as well. That rocking horse was no little toy; it was strong enough to carry my weight without breaking, and my mother had brought it from Mexico because you couldn't find things like that in New York. I can only imagine the trouble she must have had trying to check it in on the flight as part of the baggage. When I was younger, I used it all the time, especially for watching television while I rocked back and forth in the saddle, but I lost interest in it as I got older, when I became far more entertained by the electric cars that skidded around my bedroom floor, or the Walt Disney picture puzzles that I spent hours piecing together. In any case, my mother stored the horse for a long time in that forgotten corner of my bedroom, preserving it as one of the most valuable souvenirs of my childhood even after I had grown up, finished high school, moved out and left for college.

How can I describe what my mother was to me in those years? I suppose that the sense of protective strength and total intimacy that you feel for your mother as a small child is common to most if not all children. The fact of having been a part of your mother, of having lived inside her womb, of being fed from her breast, the pleasure of sucking at her nipples and tasting warm milk, the warmth of her lap and the proximity of her body are the most intense pleasures of those months that constitute the prologue to life. But every individual is unique and unrepeatable, and each personal experience belongs to that person alone. What happened to me I could never truly share with another. But I'm going to tell my story.

My mother was beautiful, with that wild beauty still notable among the women of northern Mexico. When I was a child in elementary school, she had huge dark eyes, with arching eyebrows like the wings of a crow, and lashes so thick that they could not hold the weight of makeup. They were brilliant, smoldering eyes with an inescapable magnetism that wrapped me up in their gaze and filled me with an unshakeable sense of security. While my mother was watching me, my world was perfect. There was nothing to fear. When she laughed, I felt a sense of joy that overflowed from my heart until it burst through my ribcage. But if my mother was sad, I could not bear her anguish. Maybe that's why, even now, I shrink away from the memory of her crying.

Her personality, although I didn't realize it back then, was extremely unstable. There were glorious days when the sound of her singing would wake me, as she shuffled cheerfully around the kitchen preparing breakfast, singing the songs of Alvaro Carrillo and Armando Manzanero in a voice that rose immaculate above the racket of a city morning. I would watch her with her jet black hair falling down over her cheekbones, and wait with longing for her to call me to the table. Her happiness would fill every corner of the apartment, and I felt as if I were floating in a cloud of pleasure. But then suddenly and without warning, she would see some disagreeable incident on TV, or fall out of the rhythm of her routine or recall some past failure, and her mood would change abruptly, her expression would darken, she would pull back her cheeks in an expression of annoyance, let out a sigh of resignation and sink into a taciturn silence, accompanied by the smoke of her cigarettes and slow sips from her coffee.

That ill-fated day when she took me shopping at Macy's stands out in my memory. It began as one of those days of utter joy; she had enough money to buy the dresses and blouses she wanted, and she was radiant with the anticipation of quenching her consumer thirst. She led me by the hand through every corner of the store as she looked over countless sizes and colors of dresses, different styles of leather jackets, and various designs of handbags. That was Macy's: there were items to satisfy every taste, and the offers had the appearance of a buffet. My mother loved to add to her wardrobe whenever she could, as I recall. But in the midst of her shopping frenzy I slipped from her hand without her realizing and walked off on my own. I wandered through the aisles of the store as if I were in a maze, and, deciding to play hide-and-seek, I slipped into a rack of ladies' nightgowns. Probably among those garments were some of the costliest designer labels, but of course I had no idea. While I was fully ensconced in my game, my mother became aware of my absence, and within seconds of searching she was beside herself. *"Hijo! Hijito!!"* she cried out, with her heart in her throat; I heard the alarm in her voice as something natural, like a variation on one of her songs, and I felt as if the tone of her voice was enveloping me warmly like water in a bathtub. I was blissfully unaware that she was falling into an abyss of impotence, that my absence was constricting her throat with a force greater than Mr. Morrison would ever have had in his hands, and that her desperation was clouding her reason. I was merely enjoying the game. Which is why I was struck dumbfounded when one of the store attendants discovered me in my hiding place and glared at me in silence with an expression that could have melted ice. Then he called to my mother in a feigned British accent, saying: "Here is the baby, madam," and blocked my path when I tried to escape from the tangled web of clothing. My mother appeared, her face bright red like a light bulb, her eyes popping out wildly from her head, her nostrils flaring like those of a cartoon bull, and her trembling lips spitting foam. Without saying a word, she seized my arm with a force that could have crushed the iron clothes-rack as if it were a lemon. The game was quite definitely over. At that moment, I absorbed into every pore of my being the fury of my mother. It was like a hurricane destroying trees and houses in its path, with a ferocious howl that curdled the blood. I was seized by an immeasurable terror, without limits. Years later, when I experienced the horror of a real hurricane on the coast of Florida, the panic that beset me was anchored in that primordial memory of the day I hid amidst the mountain of clothes at Macy's. There is nothing that can be compared, for a child of such a tender age, to the biblical terror unleashed by a mother's fit of rage.

3

I OWE MY life to my mother.

What I have just written is not a conventional statement, a commonplace that most people use to refer to the fact that their mother conceived them and carried them in her womb, fed them with her milk, protected them from the dangers of the world, tucked them in at night and watched over them while they slept. No, I owe my life to my mother because she saved it twice. Or, more precisely, once she saved me from losing a leg, and the other time she saved my life itself.

The day she saved my life was a New Year's Eve in Times Square. I was nine years old, and a student at an elementary school in the Bronx along with the other Mexican and black kids, and some classmates had convinced me to meet them in Manhattan's most famous square to see in the New Year. A lot of kids from the school were going because a traditional New Year's Eve party of massive proportions would be taking place there, with fireworks, cheering in the streets, and a whole lot of hoopla. They said that it was the custom to see in the New Year with a countdown, as if it were the explosion of a time bomb, and that when the clock struck twelve the night would fill with screams of joy and spectacular lights. I had naïvely agreed to meet up with another child in my class, as if in the midst of the wild frenzy it would be possible to spot a familiar face.

As I recall, when we arrived there was such a crowd that we couldn't even get off the subway at Times Square Station; we had to stay on until 8th Avenue Station, and on the walk back towards the square along 42nd Street the spectacle of the sex trade struck me for the first time. "*Girls! Girls! Girls!*" screamed the phosphorescent signs, and in the doors of each establishment stood an army of pimps and pubescent girls who served as bait for the unsuspecting tourists. Inside these establishments, in tiny rooms (I found out later) there were peepholes for spying on the shapely buttocks and erotic movements of the girls. And for fifty cents extra, you could put your hands through the holes and touch their breasts. This was in the old days, of course, because later Disney and Warner Brothers moved in with their mountains of money and set up their kids' fantasy stores in the places where the bawdy dives once offered unrestricted pleasure to the voyeurs, and the figures of Donald Duck and Sylvester the Cat permanently replaced the young beauties with their rhythmic pubes and exposed chests.

At any rate, on that night we hurried past those dens of pleasure, in a rush to reach the intersection of Broadway and Seventh Avenue in time for the final countdown, and when we got to the square there was a whir of excitement: people in stylish overcoats were uncorking champagne bottles, couples were kissing in the midst of the jostling crowds, groups of youths were swaying and singing tunes from *Godspell*, Santa Clauses were shaking bells out of time, ragged old men were begging for change, and police officers were tapping their clubs against the palms of their hands, ready to jump to action when necessary.

That night there was no violence more serious than the inevitable pushing and shoving of the crowds. The final countdown began as the human tide rocked in rhythmic waves, and I watched the fireworks with a feeling of exaltation which, judging by a photo taken of us that night, was reflected in my eyes. Five, four, three, two, one! The New Year took off with an explosion of colors in the sky, thousands of embraces were exchanged on the sidewalks of Broadway, and this euphoria took hold of everyone present to varying degrees. I began to suffocate when the people crowded together on 41st Street, forced back by a fireworks explosion that thrust bodies away in concentric circles, and on seeing my twisted expression of anguish my mother lifted me up and carried me out of the crush and towards the subway.

An air of festivity and hubbub pervaded the platform of Times Square Station, but as the party had only just begun there were not many passengers on their way home. The station was far from empty, but in spite of the crowds there were some open spaces to walk. My mother pulled me by the hand towards the front of the platform, and in that moment a child chasing another knocked into me as she ran while looking behind her. I lost my balance, and the force of the blow broke the hold that my mother had on my hand. Just as the train announced its arrival at the station with its whistle, I slid off the platform and fell headfirst onto the tracks. Onlookers screamed, I remember perfectly, and in a heartbeat my mother hurled herself off the platform, collapsed for a moment onto the tracks, wrapped her arm around my torso, and, with a strength that should have been beyond her, lifted me back onto the platform, where she fell on top of me, embracing me just in the moment that the train passed by at a murderous velocity. When people gathered round to help us, my mother fainted, and I began to cry while my heart pounded at the bars of my ribcage.

4

I BELIEVE THAT what happened to me later can be explained by the sense of security and confidence that I enjoyed in those years. My mother and I lived inside a glass bubble in which only we two existed. It was as if we formed an indestructible unit. My mother and me. I could recognize this symbiosis clearly in the mirror when she brushed my hair. In the reflection I saw an image of utter bliss, untarnished by the slightest doubt. I stood with a towel around my neck and observed my head with my hair neatly swept forward over my forehead like a newly ploughed field. My mother maneuvered the comb with a precision developed from years of routine. She parted my hair skillfully, sweeping one quarter towards the left, three quarters towards the right, and then brushed the fringe back from my forehead in a style that I had seen in pictures of the U.S. Marines. Her mastery with the comb was preceded by a light anointing with a handful of hair-gel, a viscous goo that left my hair stiff and neat. I saw the reflection of her face in the mirror as she devoted herself to the task of styling my hair, I felt the tips of her fingers as they ran over my scalp and the nape of my neck, and I believed her dedication to be indisputable proof of maternal love.

With each passing day, the conviction grew within me that my mother would spare no effort to assure my well-being. Her concern for me went far beyond waking me to school each morning, washing and ironing my clothes, preparing my meals, helping me with my homework in the evenings and taking me to Coney Island on holidays. No, she did not limit herself to the routine conventions of motherly care. She thought about me constantly, she watched over my every movement and even when she was physically far away I sensed her at my side. She knew about all that I did and all that I left undone, all that I thought and all that I felt, all that I wished for and all that I feared. Her shadow followed me by day and her spirit visited me in my dreams.

In reality, I was never alone. The day I suffered the most serious accident of my existence she came running to my side to help me. It was a Friday after school, and the sunset was reflected on the waters of the East River. I was standing in front of the trunk of a car, one of those Ford Thunderbirds that were everywhere in the days when big cars were still in fashion, and I held the basketball that my friends and I were using to practice our slam-dunks in the dying light of the day. Night was drawing in and most of the kids on the team had already gone home. The only two left were Jonathan, who stood waiting for me to pass him the ball, and me. I was simply killing time because I knew that in a few minutes Julie, Jonathan's twin sister, would arrive. His mother would arrive too of course, but it was Julie who interested me. At the age of thirteen, I was still not quite in the full bloom of sexual awakening, but I liked the girl all the same. I liked to look at her; that was all. She was blonde, with a church angel face, Shirley Temple curls, and eyes of a blue so clear that they seemed to gaze at me from the other side of the sky.

Seeing that Julie still hadn't arrived, I raised the ball above my head to toss it to Jonathan, and in that moment a truck smashed violently into a dark green car (I remember it perfectly) which in turn came crashing into the trunk of the parked Thunderbird, trapping my right leg in the melee. What happened next I don't recall, because I was knocked out by the impact. I lost consciousness immediately, but I was later told that Jonathan's mother took me to the nearest hospital. Two medics on duty examined me in the emergency room, and came to the rash decision that my leg would have to be amputated. According to their diagnosis, my thigh was in such a bad state that it might quickly turn gangrenous, and the infection would spread to my groin and take my life in no time.

As time is a very important factor in surgery, the medics went to work at once, and just as they were preparing me for an emergency operation my mother stormed into the hospital. She arrived in a rage, from what I heard. She wanted to know who had been responsible for the accident so that she could gouge out his eyes with her fingernails, and she was deadly serious. When she was told of the operation about to be performed, she lost it totally. She grabbed Jonathan's mother by the lapels of her coat and shouted in her face that no son-of-a-bitch doctor was going to cut off her only son's leg. Fortunately, she said all this in Spanish, so Jonathon's mother had no idea what she was saying. She then barged into the operating room without authorization, and when she couldn't find me anywhere she smashed a bottle of serum against the medicine cabinet. It was quite the scandal. Security were on the scene in a matter of seconds, and my mother threatened to burn the hospital down if they didn't return her son to her with both legs intact. I am grateful to have been sleeping during this whole scene.

When they brought my mother to my side, she told one of the doctors, in a slightly calmer tone, that she did not authorize any amputation whatsoever. She called for the intervention of Jose Luis Orbea, a doctor of Basque origin who had treated her some years earlier when she had broken her wrist falling over in the bathtub, and his second opinion was that my body required a strong dose of antibiotics to attack the infection, but that my leg could be saved. A meticulous thighbone reconstruction operation and probably a small prosthesis would see me walking again. The medics who were preparing to operate were thus left with their gloves on and their handsaw sharpened, poised for the next victim of their ineptitude.

Now that I look at my whole leg, I touch my thigh and the scar left by that incident, I think of the miles I have jogged, the mornings when I have jumped out of bed, the basketball games, the walks along the Seine and through Central Park, the cities I have wandered around on foot, the ski-trips to Montramblanc, the ability to step on the gas in a car or the simple and wondrous pleasure of contemplating the world on my feet, with the natural strength of both my legs, and I feel a profound gratitude to the woman who made it all possible.

5

I HAVE LATELY begun to question just how well a man can ever come to know his mother. I mean, to really know her. The small child knows nothing about her. He simply senses her, enjoys or endures her presence, and tests out her different moods. He monitors her, you might say. When the child is alone – absorbed in his games – and his mother suddenly appears, he knows by the simple tone of her voice whether she is happy, sad, contented or angry; he knows whether she has come to scold him for misbehaving, or to embrace him for no apparent reason. He even knows, although he understands it only on a confused level, if his mother is sad in spite of her smile, if she is filled with a deep resentment, or if she is acting kindly only to clear her conscience of guilt. The child possesses an innate ability to discern any falsehood. He knows if he is loved unconditionally, if he is being rejected for some hidden reason or if his existence is of no consequence. Every child has an internal thermometer to measure the degrees of warmth and affection he receives.

What the child does not know, and the adult comes to know only partially, is the true identity of this person who cared for him, fed him, pampered him, repressed him, encouraged him to grow and subtly domesticated him in his childhood. Any son can describe his own mother, without doubt, and even the most uptight individual knows her pleasures, her whims and her aversions. But there is always a shadow of doubt, an unknown territory that is closed over like a scar, which proves impassable for any child.

There are a multitude of questions that any son might ask himself about his own mother that may not be easy to answer. Who really is my mother? What was her life like before I came into it? Was she a happy child? Was she loved by her parents? Did she get what she had hoped for out of life? Did she truly love my father? Did she give herself freely to him in the moment that I was conceived? Did she really love the fruit of her womb? Or did she see me as a burden, a responsibility that life had thrust upon her without ever asking her if she was ready for it?

My mother was a waitress in diners and restaurants. That was her trade. She worked in all kinds of places, from cleaning the Formica tables in a Taco Bell in Queens to taking orders on roll-er-skates in a pizzeria with long corridors in the heart of Little Italy. As she was dedicated and responsible, in time she came to work at the Grand Central Oyster Bar, a restaurant with a better reputation and a fast customer turnover, where they served a clam chowder that seemed to me the most exquisite dish in the universe.

I have already mentioned that my mother was very attractive, with a beauty that resembled the Mexican movie starlets of the forties, and her raven black mane of hair was an additional attraction for the customers who would watch her as she brought the dishes to their tables. But as far as I knew, she never came to establish any kind of relationship with any of the regulars. I'm not referring here merely to amorous relationships; the fact is, I never knew of a single friend or acquaintance of hers who had ever been a customer in any restaurant where she had provided her services.

I don't mean to suggest that my mother was an anti-social, excessively picky or aloof woman. It could be said that she was a person who was open to the possibility of establishing new relationships. She was always friendly with my friends' mothers, although she never had the time to go out for lunch or coffee with them because at any moment when she was not with me she was invariably working. She never realized it, but she was popular in the neighborhood, mainly due to an episode in which she played a central role, and which I will recount later. First, however, I want to introduce one Señor Agustin Miranda, an individual who I now understand was implicated in the events that were to unfold many years later.

This Señor Miranda had a very special relationship with my mother. He was not what you would call a suitor, boyfriend or lover; on the many occasions I saw them together, not once did they seem to share any kind of intimacy. He was much older than she was, and she once told me that she had been her favorite teacher when she was young. Before we came to New York, even before I was born, my mother had in fact studied Political Science at the University of Mexico, where, she told me, she had learned to analyze the complexities of the world. Unfortunately, once she got to Manhattan she forgot everything she'd learned in her studies because they were of no use to her here at all. The only activity that she continued without a pause was her painting. As a result, our apartment had no living room for receiving visitors, as in the space adjacent to the dining room she had set up her studio, filled with canvases, paintings and easels. There she would spend long evenings sketching or painting dreamy landscapes, portraits and profiles of women vanishing into the wind, horses galloping across fields, and inscrutable visions, many of them horrific. Some of her pictures frightened me in the daytime and kept me awake at night. Sometimes she would show me a book of the works of Leonora Carrington, which only added to my confusion. Señor Miranda, on the other hand, liked her pictures. Or rather, he used them as an excuse to talk about other matters. On the occasions when he came to our apartment the two of them would go into the studio, and my mother would begin to draw the images that haunted her dreams, while Señor Miranda would sit on a stool to exchange platitudes until the early hours of the morning. He always spoke in Spanish (I remember because his voice was very deep, like the voice of a radio announcer) but they spoke of topics so abstract that I have forgotten them completely. Their conversations often consisted of little more than the simple exchange of monosyllables, and on saying goodbye they merely shook hands with the coolness of neighbors who had only just met.

One memorable night, shortly after the departure of Señor Miranda, I woke up in fright. I remember on that day, by pure coincidence, I had come across a magazine in the diner a block and a half away from our apartment. As I thumbed through it, I stumbled on an article that caught my eye for its dramatic content; it presented, in a grand photographic display, all of the suicide victims who had thrown themselves from the top of the Empire State Building, in those days the tallest building in the world. There were appalling images of bodies hurling towards death, and interviews with the pedestrians who had suffered the misfortune of crossing the street on the corner of Fifth Avenue and 34th Street right at the precise moment when a body fell and splattered on the pavement. I imagined the shock, the astonishment, the distress, the horror of witnessing a death so brutal and unexpected.

Then that night, I heard my mother screaming: "Mrs. Wharton! Mrs. Wharton!" and moments later she rushed into my room, scooped me up into her arms and ran out of the apartment, and flew down the stairs for no apparent reason, only to race back up to our floor the moment she had left me in my pajamas in the open air of the street. I had no idea what was happening; nobody had told me that there was a fire in Mrs. Wharton's apartment. A spark from an electric plug had set a tablecloth aflame in her living room, and while Mrs. Wharton slept soundly in her bedroom a cloud of smoke billowed out under the doors, and the fire scaled the wooden shelves where she kept her books and pictures.

Wendy and Pimpinela, her two little watchdogs, raised the alarm. My mother heard their barking while she was setting her alarm clock before getting into bed. She ran out at once into the corridor, and on seeing the smoke seeping out under our neighbor's front door she began to bang at it in exasperation and urgency.

From the street below I could see a pillar of smoke wafting out of Mrs. Wharton's living-room window, giving the building an even more gloomy quality than usual. Little by little, the neighbors became aware of the fire and started emerging in a procession from the building. The first out were the Manleys. This was in the days when their father still lived with them, and they followed him towards the exit without the boisterous racket that was their trademark. The boys were clearly frightened, and set against the smoke rising up the walls and the darkness of the night they looked strangely pale. Then came many neighbors unknown to me; some I had seen before briefly passing to their respective floors, others I had never seen before at all. Among them were two effeminate men who were no doubt compelled to hide their inclinations in an era when homosexuality was not openly expressed as it is now, and a couple of Arabic appearance who emerged with a boy who must have been about my age, who, like all those present, failed to understand what was happening, with the additional aggravation (I realize now) that he was a Down Syndrome child. At the time, I remember the sunken form of his eyes, but New York had such a huge jumble of races that I imagined that they merely represented another variant of the physiognomy of Asian children, already present in large numbers in those days.

The firemen arrived just at the moment that Mr. Morrison came hobbling out the front door of the building supported on a pair of crutches, and they immediately raised a tall ladder towards the window of Mrs. Wharton. Their handiwork was a captivating spectacle for the children who watched, although for me it was not quite so absorbing. The only thing that concerned me at that moment was the whereabouts of my mother. I did not understand why she had left me alone in the middle of the street, or why she had gone back inside the building. The neighbors didn't seem to notice her absence. Only Mr. Morrison, who had staggered gasping to the fender of a car parked in front of the building, began to shout with what air remained in his lungs that my mother was still inside, that she had knocked down the door of Mrs. Wharton's apartment with an axe, and that he had seen her disappear into the cloud of smoke that filled the hallway of our floor.

Hearing his words, I dimly understood that my mother would surely die inside, and I shot straight for the front door of the building. I didn't know whether I wanted to save her or die with her, but I felt it imperative to be at her side. At that moment I felt a strong grip that stopped me in my tracks. One of the firemen held me back, extinguishing my momentum even as it ignited, and tried to calm me down with his firm voice. In that same moment I saw my mother emerge from the building, struggling to hold up Mrs. Wharton, whose considerable girth constituted an added hindrance to the rescue mission. My mother stepped out into the cold street with a damp handkerchief over her mouth, and Mrs. Wharton came hugging a shopping bag in which her dogs sat shuddering.

That night we slept at the fire station, and my mother became the heroine of the barrio. All of the neighbors looked at her with genuine admiration and affection. In the midst of the chaos and confusion of the fire, she had been the only person with the wherewithal to break into Mrs. Wharton's apartment and lead her out of the inferno, dogs and all. When we arrived at the station, Mr. Manley, who barely greeted my mother when he saw her in the hallway, came to her somewhat timidly and covered her with a blanket. Mrs. Manley watched her in silence, with a look of the utmost respect. Even Mr. Morrison, always so antisocial and unpredictable in his choleric outbursts, came to her side and whispered something into her ear. My mother simply nodded and smiled gratefully.

Although the incident did not receive the attention accorded to the tragedies that occurred periodically in the Bowery district or by the pier, its impact attracted reporters from the local radio station, who arrived at the fire station the following morning. They came in noisily, wielding microphones and tape recorders, and at once began to take testimonies from the neighbors and the firemen. In describing the details of the fire, all of the witnesses coincided in the opinion that my mother was the heroine of the night… which was the last thing in the world that she could possibly have wanted. When she saw a photographer approach her pointing the lens of his camera in her direction, she covered her face to block the light of the flash, and then when a reporter moved towards her with his tape recorder for an interview, she took me by the arm almost violently and dragged me out of the station, evading a threat far more harrowing to her than the flames of the fire.

What was my mother running from? She was hardly an inhibited individual. But she certainly had her reserved side. I had always been aware that she didn't like to be talked about. She was never drawn to the spotlight. She liked to watch spectacles, not to be the subject of them. Now I understand why; but at that moment, the only thing I understood was that fame was not to her taste.

"Why did we leave the firemen, mama?" I asked her ingenuously.

"We are going home, *mi amor*," was how she answered. It was the first time that she had ever spoken to me in English.

And that is exactly what we did. Our apartment had not been affected by the fire, and once the police cordon had been removed all the residents of the building were able to return to their respective homes. Mrs. Wharton used some of her savings to pay some boys who helped her remove the wood and ash from the burned chairs and bookcases, and the only traces remaining of the fire were the smoke-stained walls around her window facing the street.

In the weeks after the fire, and until a heart attack took her from the building once and for all, Mrs. Wharton would leave my mother a bunch of flowers at the foot of our front door every day, as a small tribute to her bravery and generosity. She bought them at the florist on the corner, run by a Chinese man with eyes like coin slots. In the beginning, out of embarrassment or modesty, my mother tried to return the flowers. But Mrs. Wharton persisted in delivering these gestures of her gratitude, a feeling that had the positive effect of bringing her out of her isolation. It was as if at the end of her life she had acknowledged the existence of good will among human beings. After a few days, my mother began accepting her daily tribute, and on several occasions I noticed her holding the carnations to her nose and savoring their sweet fragrance. Yet in spite of such gratuitous pleasure, I can testify to the fact that the fame thrust upon her as a result of her heroic act in that fire never went to her head.

6

MY MOTHER WAS always present in my dreams. In the beginning, I couldn't distinguish the waking world very well from the dream world. At night, my mother would come to my bed, lie down with me a moment, make the sign of the cross over me, caress my hair for a long time, kiss me on the cheek, and then turn out the light and leave the room quietly, leaving me in a placid state resembling that of the saints on the doors of Saint Patrick's. Then I would drift slowly into the world of dreams, where my mother would return to take part in my adventures.

I had a recurring dream, with certain variations, which was as thrilling as it was torturous. First, I would find myself in a junk-yard, a depressing site resembling the car cemetery that I saw the first time we went to New Jersey. It was a squalid and desolate place, filled with empty cans, used tires and all kinds of discarded junk. There, in the midst of so much garbage, I felt completely lost. I was alone, disoriented, hopeless, feeling incapable of escape. I can even still recall the pestilent smell of the trash (something unusual for a dream) as something like the odor of the slaughter-houses that used to be located outside Queens. This meant that I not only felt helpless, but found myself on the verge of throwing up.

Then, like an angel descended from heaven, my mother would appear on top of a garbage heap, dressed up as if she were on her way to a gala ball. She wore a blue dress with veils, and I would watch her extending her arms towards me, calling my name as if I had just come out of school. From that moment, I could feel my expression brighten. I would start shouting: "Mama! I'm coming! I'm coming right away!" And as I bounded towards her over the piles of refuse, the scenery would begin to change, gloriously transformed in rhythm to my running. First, a few plants would appear, sprouting up from the quagmire of trash and growing with amazing speed, turning into the robust trees of Park Avenue as I passed them; then the elms of Central Park would appear, and around the heaps of scrap metal and squashed cardboard boxes would appear the outlines of the buildings that surround the park like sentinels: the Dakota, with its symmetrical windows and ochre colors; the Hotel Plaza, with its renaissance façade; the Twin Towers of the thirties, with that grace granted only by the passage of time. I would regard this fantastic metamorphosis with a joy that knew no bounds; I would look to my mother in the distance and run towards her embrace with renewed resolve, while the city grew up all around me as if by magic. It was an extraordinary sensation; I felt as if wings sprouted from my shoulder blades, and I began to fly unhindered through the avenues and alleyways. Then the widest path in the junkyard turned into Broadway, the shattered windscreens were transformed into brilliant neon signs dancing with light, the skeleton of a dilapidated truck expanded suddenly to take on the dimensions of Radio City, the puddles of putrid water crystallized into the skating rink of the Rockefeller Center, and all at once the city rose up with its colossal buildings and filled up with its inhabitants from every corner of the world. The Avenue of the Americas was flooded with a procession of Africans, Jews, Chinese, Italians, Koreans, Polish, Puerto Ricans, Greeks and Russians, and a sensation of joy overflowed like a river in flood when I reached my mother and her figure fused with mine in an embrace, and then I understood that it was not really my mother that I was hugging, but the city that was my mother protector, my womb of safety and my daily nourishment, that kept me on solid ground with the serene majesty of her bridges and wrapped me up seductively in the monumental strength of her towers and skyscrapers.

Then I would wake up and find myself looking into my mother's enormous eyes, which looked down on me with that assurance of safety that filled me with a bliss that I cannot describe precisely, but which I still long for desperately when I lay awake at night, and which I regain only very occasionally in my dreams.

7

MANY YEARS LATER, one fateful Monday, my belief was confirmed that New York was truly the capital of the world. It was the fall of 1987. My mother had just bought a small house in the suburbs of Brooklyn, and I had reached the appropriate age for the odd girlfriend or two. The streets of the city were strewn with fallen leaves and the sunsets painted brightly colored designs on the most beautiful buildings on Manhattan's south side. I was working at a magazine store on the days I didn't have school, and I had raised enough money to go see Madonna at Madison Square Garden. In those days, AIDS was claiming the lives of dozens of artists of Hollywood and the Village, and Madonna had organized a concert to raise funds to help find a cure for this modern plague. Her shows were also peppered with social and political critiques; as she sang "Papa Don't Preach", the image of Ronald Reagan appeared on a huge screen above the stage, and at the end of the song his face dissolved into a caption that read: "Safe Sex". The audience was electrified by the high-voltage intensity that rocked the stage with sound and light, and Madonna's pelvic thrusts declared an end to Republican conservatism in this Mecca of modern capitalism. Meanwhile, on the other side of the world,

Mikhail Gorbachev was dynamiting the elephantine armature of the Soviet regime with his reformist ideals.

Then suddenly, the course of history took an abrupt turn. Without warning, the New York Stock Market plummeted with all the clamor and expansive force that the power of money can exert. That tiny alley called Wall Street shook with a financial tremor measuring several points on the Richter scale, and its aftershocks rocked every corner of the world. On the news they announced that the Dow Jones Index had dropped by over five hundred points in a single day, representing the evaporation of five hundred billion dollars, an amount equivalent to all the wealth produced by France in a year. *Ka-pow!* I did not understand the significance of such a figure, but from the graphic language of the stockbrokers I deduced that we were witnessing a global catastrophe of cataclysmic proportions. And in effect that is what it was; on the TV screens appeared a parade of terrified faces of Germans, Koreans, Australians, Spaniards, Mexicans, Italians, Brazilians, Indians, Israelis and Canadians. The horror had left its mark on all the faces of all those who had seen their money vanish overnight, and the devastation had made no national distinctions. Neither had it shown any respect for racial or social hierarchy: the depression equally affected black and white, rich and poor. What was certain was that millions of families had lost their inheritance in a matter of minutes. It was a modern tragedy. There were people who also lost their heads in their personal downward spirals into desperation. In Miami, an investor took his life with a well-aimed bullet, after killing his financial advisor in a fit of rage. In Manhattan, people went on wild shopping sprees, withdrawing all their savings in response to the impotent paranoia in financial circles. The world was a mess, and it was New York's fault.

A week after the Wall Street debacle, the Andersons came to dinner at our house. Their visits were routine, because my mother was a cook of considerable resources. She had learned to whip up dishes of almost every national cuisine of the world, having worked as a waitress in Chinese, Italian, Thai, German, Tex-Mex, and, of course, Mexican restaurants. Her intelligence and skill enabled her to learn quickly. She knew how to make chop suey, paella Valencia, butter fettuccini and pozole. The Andersons loved her pozole. They ate it up eagerly, enduring the spiciness of the chili that set their taste buds on fire. They had to drink gallons of water to counteract the effects, but they always asked for more. Their taste for spice made them insatiable, and while he sweated from the sweet sting of the chili Mr. Anderson chatted away like a whirlwind; about what was happening in the neighborhood, about his cousins in Iowa, about the constantly increasing pace of daily life. He would then ask bravely for another pozole, and my mother would serve him as if he were a *compadre* from the homeland.

That night, the Andersons arrived in a very bad mood, which was not at all typical of them. Mrs. Anderson, who was on more intimate terms with my mother, sat down on the main sofa in the living room, stretched out her septuagenarian arm to show off her cheap imitation jewelry, and without further preambles announced:

"We're flat broke."

Like many couples over retirement age, the Andersons lived off their income from social security and the interest from their modest investments in the stock market. Mr. Anderson had been a math teacher in various high schools and his wife had worked as floor manager in a K-Mart. Since their retirement, the dream of their lives had been to move to a house with a yard of sufficient size for their four dogs. Their policy of systematic saving had deprived them of several vacations on the Mexican beaches where they used to go on package deals, but had allowed them to raise enough money to pay the deposit on a good sized house in South Brooklyn. But then the unexpected stock market collapse cut down their income by more than half, and overnight they found themselves in the sorry situation of having to reduce expenses with painful alternatives for a couple accustomed to a particular way of life: they could lower their mortgage payments, or stop eating out or going to the movies, or limit their spending on medication (Mr. Anderson suffered from hypertension and Mrs. Anderson from bouts of severe depression), or they could get rid of the dogs. To add insult to injury, David – their only son – had lost his job as a mechanic with General Motors while in the midst of a messy divorce involving two children. This meant that their son not only could not help out his parents in their plight, but that his situation put them under pressure to offer him economic assistance. In this state of emergency, they had opted for keeping the house and giving away their dogs. It was a painful choice, because pets tend to mean more to most Americans than do their children.

After dinner, when we all retired to the living room, my mother excused herself for a moment and stepped quietly up the recently carpeted stairs to her room. Mrs. Anderson lit a cigarette, lifted her gaze to the roof and lost herself in her daydreams. Seeing that we had effectively been left alone, Mr. Anderson fixed me with a predator's glare. I smiled at him in self-defense, without knowing exactly what I was defending myself against. Perhaps he detected my helplessness, as he was evidently preparing for a calculated strike that would put my manhood to the test.

"How are the magazine sales going?" He threw out the question as if it were a shiny bait on a hook.

"Fine, Mr. Anderson, thank you," I answered, disconcerted by the razor sharpness of his gaze. "Luckily, there are customers for every kind..."

"For every kind!" he interjected with a voice that sounded like the roar of a jet en route to La Guardia. "Don't tell me they've got *every kind* of magazine for sale!"

His remark left me petrified. I felt exposed, as if I had been caught committing a heinous crime. Suffice it to say that Mr. Anderson's philosophical principles were the total opposite of the liberty and rebellion that filled the air at a Madonna concert.

Mr. Anderson knew perfectly well that the magazine store where I worked sold the *New York Times* and *Washington Post*, the international and economic news magazines, entertainment weeklies, sports, automobile, women's fashion and fitness magazines, as well as *Playboy* and *Penthouse*, and countless "underground" publications. I felt as if my flesh were burning with shame.

"There are some publications that..." he made a very prolonged pause, as if searching for the right word, "...that show the darker side of things, what lies beneath the surface..."

Then, as his wife had thrown her head back and closed her eyes in an expression of utter disinterest in our conversation, Mr. Anderson did something that I never would have imagined from a Republican of his ilk; from his jacket pocket he took out a playing card with the figure of a naked woman on the front, and he showed it to me with a wink. It was barely a fraction of a second, and when my mother came out of her bedroom to return to the discussion, Mr. Anderson had recovered his customary composure.

As if nothing had happened, my mother and Mrs. Anderson began to talk of recipes, as they did habitually. My mother explained to her the art of making eggplant with olive oil, chicken parmesan, cheese-filled zucchini, spicy tabouli, steak with soy sauce, and, most importantly, mole poblano, which she only ever spoke of theoretically, because the huge quantity of ingredients of that delicious Mexican specialty could only be obtained south of the Rio Grande.

These prolonged culinary conversations visibly bored Mr. Anderson, and taking advantage of a phone call from his son he slipped out to the back yard to talk in private. This interval was sufficient for Mrs. Anderson to lean towards my mother and tell her, in a confidential tone:

"George is going insane. We don't have enough money for his blood-pressure pills, so he's bought himself a bunch of do-it-yourself anti-stress meditation books, and he spends the whole day monitoring the rhythm of his breath with his eyes closed… he hides the monthly mortgage payment bills from me, and his new obsession is making lists of names of stock brokers who, according to him, were to blame for the Wall Street disaster. It's a total nightmare… most of the time we don't even have anything to eat in the house."

Without uttering a single word, my mother took a folded yellow envelope out of her jacket pocket, and with a benevolent smile handed it to Mrs. Anderson, who opened it to discover a clutch of fifty- and hundred-dollar bills inside. She closed up the envelope again and returned it to my mother with a blush.

"I can't accept it" she said, her eyes going moist, "surely, you're as poor as we are…"

"Don't accept it," answered my mother, "think of it like a loan from a bank… you've accepted bank loans before, haven't you? Well, this is just the same… except that I won't send you bank statements… Look, Claire," (this was Mrs. Anderson's first name) "you're a believer, and you know very well that the Lord never leaves His children abandoned… I am only an instrument, and it is He Who moves me to help you… Besides, I don't even need it… one of the advantages of being a foreigner is that I can't invest in the stock market. I keep my savings in an old-fashioned piggy-bank, so financial crises don't affect me…"

That day I learned, among other things, that my mother not only possessed the generosity of a saint, but also the kind of financial savvy that Donald Trump would have given his eye teeth for.

8

WHEN I FIRST met Samantha, I was still being held hostage to
the dubious virtues of chastity. I am not so sure if she was too,
although it is likely. I was seventeen years old, and she was just a
little bit older, but in the field of relations with the opposite sex
she held a notable advantage over me. I had not had a stable relationship with any girl in my adolescence, although there were
many who had caught my eye. Samantha had had a boyfriend
some years earlier with all the formality that her fifteen summers
had demanded, a boy who had been her childhood friend and ultimately her high school prom date. She swore to me, nevertheless,
that in their intimate moments they had never crossed the fron-
tier of exploring one another's bodies with hands and mouths.

Samantha was a typical girl of Irish stock whose ancestors
had been among those poor huddled masses who had sailed to
Manhattan's hopeful shore in the middle of the nineteenth century. She was as white as the foam of the sea, with wavy chestnut
hair and skin spattered with freckles. She had eyes as large and
lively as those of the squirrels in the Park, and a nose that seemed
to sharpen with every smile. It was her smile that I liked most
about her, as it had a character that was not merely joyful, but
brimming with mischief. As I was a tall and lanky youth, she nick-

named me *Javelin*. "Fly, Javelin, fly!" she would call to me, challenging me to chase her as she ran along the serpentine pathways of Central Park.

I met Samantha in the magazine store one day during lunch hour when there were no customers. She came in wearing flared pants and a blouse with the ends tied together just above her bellybutton. I was too bashful to do more than steal sideways glances while she leafed through a magazine. But these brief glances were enough to discern one of her interests from the cover of the magazine in her hands.

"You like ice-skating then?" I asked her in what was almost a whisper.

As a facility for talking to strangers was one of her virtues, my question was the initiation of a highly animated conversation in which she confessed to me that figure-skating was her passion and that her role model was Katarina Witt, a beautiful skating champion born in East Germany, who lived in a development of grey and gloomy buildings in East Berlin called the Karl Marx Complex.

"Can you imagine what it must be like to live in a communist country and get out and do pirouettes on ice to the music of Gershwin?" she asked me with a gaze that shone, I realized afterwards, like the blade of her skates. "Katarina has military discipline: she gets up early, goes to school in the morning, and trains until sunset. She doesn't eat ice-cream, or go to parties, or date anyone... and she skates like a goddess! She's the champion of the world!"

In that moment I didn't know whether she admired the skater for her rigor, for the music of Gershwin or for not dating, but I felt a sudden pressing need to be like Katarina Witt; not for the dexterity of her skating, nor for her discipline or fame; but simply because I wanted to be admired by this freckle-faced girl who seemed to me a slice of heaven on earth.

"I'm not dating anyone either," I said stupidly.

Samantha eyed me with a mixture of surprise and amusement. She took this puerile comment to be the wittiest of jokes, and she felt suddenly overwhelmed by a kind of empathy; in that early moment of our relationship she believed that she had discovered a soul mate, someone who also possessed that strange gift of the quick and perfect word, that combination of childish candor and biting wit that could unbalance the most artful speaker.

It is an established fact that, at seventeen, love is a Molotov cocktail with the explosive power to blow any barrier to smithereens. Samantha and I had absolutely nothing in common, and nevertheless our relationship was filled with attraction, intrigue, playfulness and vitality. The attraction of opposites, the learned would claim. A comedy of errors, the dramaturges would suggest. But more likely it was the coincidence of hopes and desires, the roulette wheel of fantasies, the ambiguous images that we create of the loved one with their resulting doses of idolatry, obsession, rejection and disappointment.

Samantha was a daughter of the upper middle-class, that pretentious group who sent their daughters to ballet school and tortured them by forcing them to analyze the works of Shakespeare and Yeats, but who could not prevent them from sliding culturally into the music of Harlem, or, worse still, into the labyrinthine specter of drugs. I came from the most depressed neighborhoods of Manhattan, I was of Mexican origin, and I carried on my back the promise of social redemption by way of personal exertion and academic achievement. Our families could not have been more different. Samantha's father was a modest though relatively prosperous industrialist who had accumulated a small fortune with a furniture factory outlet; my mother was a waitress of considerable skill, but who in reality (it pains me to acknowledge it) had never risen to the heights of *maitre d'* in a high-class establishment. Looking back, Samantha had class, faced the world in style, and was clearly destined to become the first wife of a Wall Street yuppie; I, on the other hand, as time would reveal, did not fit in anywhere, and was fated to return to Mexico.

There were, nevertheless, two shared interests that strengthened our temporary compatibility: Catholicism and dancing. It may seem trivial, but going to mass every Sunday set us apart from the black and Anglo-Saxon masses, and the Afro-Caribbean dancehalls became our mutual hangouts. I loved jazz, salsa, Willy Colon, and Chao Feliciano, and she was fascinated by the bars with velvety saxophones and melancholy piano chords, and the ballrooms filled with sequined dresses and strobes, flickering to the rhythm of the bongos with flashes of intense white light, the smell of bodies made sweaty from the dance and the sound of riotous laughter that resonated with the uninhibited freedom of the Caribbean Sea.

Ah, how we enjoyed life! It was incredible, but she thought that I was a guy of extraordinary intelligence who worked in a magazine store out of curiosity and for pleasure, but when the opportunity presented itself I would turn into a business magnate, a talented director for a major television network, a presidential campaign advisor or a PR manager with the persuasive force sufficient to convince half the world to consume nitro-glycerin instead of Prozac to combat depression. As for me, I didn't build such castles in the sky with regard to our future, but neither did I see her in any objective or realistic light. I worshipped her in a very peculiar way; I thought that her outer beauty was a completely accurate reflection of her inner bliss, and that her missionary inclinations towards the poorer sectors of the community were indicative of a kind of beatitude. We were both in love with an ingenuous mystification of the other, but this didn't stop us from enjoying the moment.

Like all good New Yorkers, we reveled together in that tapestry of everyday urban culture of which sexuality forms an inseparable part. I remember well the first kiss she gave me. It was not, to be honest, a sentimental or romantic gesture. It carried no suggestion of affection, or tenderness, or even of fondness. It was, to put it bluntly, a feminine tribute to my intellectual qualities. It may sound pretentious, but that is what it was. At the beginning of our relationship, in that interregnum during which you do your best to present only your finer qualities, we frequented museums and art galleries, which were among her passions. I didn't have the slightest idea about painting or sculpture, but I simulated a moderate interest in anything that she liked. With our student cards in hand, we entered all the most expensive museums for affordable fees. We looked over all the rooms of the Metropolitan, the Museum of Modern Art and many others besides. On one of these outings, one afternoon on the spiral ramp of the Guggenheim, we shared our first truly physical intimacy. We had just viewed her favorite works by Cezanne, Braque, Picasso, Kandinsky and Van Gogh, and wandering by one of the most popular exhibits I was particularly drawn to a Magritte painting, called *Empire of Light*. As in many of the paintings by this artist (I looked him up later), there was a strange combination of light and shade, dream and truth. In the middle of the painting appeared a house drowned in the darkness of night, illuminated faintly by a spotlight. Above the house was a sky at daytime, the clouds shining with their whiteness in a diaphanous and brilliant firmament. I lingered for some time to contemplate it, and without thinking I associated it with my shifts at the magazine store. So I said:

"That's what my work is like."

"Ah!" answered Samantha with her proverbial irony, "I didn't know that you were a painter too."

"No, I'm not. But I can make out the light of the working day, and the darkness too…"

Samantha looked at me with an expression of perplexity and rapture, as if I had just synthesized in a sentence the full depth of the painting. Then she took me by the arm, leaned her head against my shoulder, and led me to the winding ramp that identified the profile of the museum and defined its architecture. We walked out onto the balcony, where from on high we watched the people leaving the museum before closing time, and in that moment she took my face in her hand as if it were an apple and forced her tongue into my mouth vehemently, searching for something inside me that would give her the key to my sensitivity or astuteness. This sudden attack robbed me of my self-control, rendering me completely stunned, although I admit that not even in the most alert state would I have imagined that it was the preamble to what happened next.

"Catch me, Javelin!" said Samantha, and she set off running down the spiral ramp. We descended one, two, three levels at full speed, and then she stopped abruptly and backed up against the wall of the elevator, next to the women's bathroom. She pulled me towards her body and with a quick turn led me through the lavatory door. There was nobody inside; we entered one of the stalls and she began to kiss my neck, my mouth, my ears, and I responded by slipping my hand into her panties and fervently caressing that hair even fluffier than the curls that trembled on her head. She laughed and kissed me, and her mischievous laughter was so contagious that I also began to laugh, until a woman entered the restroom and Samantha hushed up, petrified by the sensation of breaking all the rules and holding her breath ecstatically while my fingers continued slowly to caress those delicate lips that opened up like a juicy peach.

Had her boyfriend touched her like this? I was so insecure in those days that this question crossed my mind at the most untimely moment, and the resultant flash of jealousy made me lose my nerve and withdraw my hand. Samantha interpreted this as an interjection of maturity in the midst of our madness. She kissed my lips with the moisture of hers, buttoned up her pants and blouse to avoid any suspicion, and left the stall to check that the coast was clear. By this time there was almost nobody left in the museum, and we left the women's bathroom together, hand in hand and with an enviable serenity, as if we had immersed ourselves the whole afternoon in the complete works of Matisse.

9

My mother had a particular affection for material things. She liked to acquire objects that she believed would be useful or enjoyable, but it was hard for her to let things go when they no longer served their purpose. To her, everything had a value. Whether the value of the object was historical, biographical or sentimental, it was worth keeping.

"They say that with time things lose their usefulness," she told me once while she was putting away her old dresses, "but I say that with time that usefulness simply changes."

In our new house in Brooklyn, her bedroom was a faithful reflection of her personality. The most important pieces of furniture in the room were those used for storage. There were wardrobes, dressers, shelves, and, most important of all, a closet protected against any outsider's intrusion, whose only key she guarded jealously. That private space, reserved exclusively for her most intimate secrets, was off limits to everybody else. Guests were allowed in the hallway, the living room or her painting studio, the dining room with its glass cases of plates and cups, my own bedroom, the strategically located bathrooms, or even the doorway to her bedroom. But beyond that point, passage was forbidden.

One day of treachery, I broke into her private territory. I was doing my homework in my bedroom, which was located at the other end of the hall on the second floor of the house, and, looking for a calculator, I wandered into her room. Between her dressers there was a table that served as a desk, and while rummaging through her belongings there I noticed that the closet door had been left ajar. My mother's closet door... ajar? My first impulse was to close it. If I had done that, I would have lived up to my self-image as the good child, obedient, submissive and incurious. But I didn't. I was seduced by indiscretion and intrigue, by the desire to cross the threshold of insubordination. I opened the closet, and, for the first time in my life, I stepped onto forbidden ground. I turned on the closet light and found myself surrounded by familiar objects that at the same time looked strange in this unfamiliar place: the uniforms my mother had used in the restaurants where she was required to wear one; the tailored dresses that she wore for special occasions, the bathrobes and nightgowns, the rows of shoes that she collected like dolls, and an array of useless objects that she kept as souvenirs – my rocking horse, her sewing-machine, a disused vacuum cleaner, a collection of irons from a bygone era and a wickerwork rocker bought from an old woman who lived in the Papaloapan River valley. At the bottom of the closet was a small chest full of drawers, and on opening the first drawer I recognized its archival value; my mother kept all her books, magazines, documents and photographs in perfect order. The books were a diverse and antiquated assortment; *Madame Bovary* next to texts on war by Clausewitz and Lenin, *War and Peace* alongside works by Leon Trotsky. There were documents too; a confused mess of papers containing political analyses of various states of Mexico, loose notes on the whereabouts of people I guessed must have been old friends, birth certificates of various people – including several copies of my own – passports of unknown women and cuttings from Mexican newspapers of different dates.

But what caught my attention most was a drawer full of photographs. You might imagine that the photos she kept were of family, of her most beloved places in Mexico, of friends or from trips taken, but no: every one of the photos was of Sophia Loren. Sophia Loren? Yes, Sophia Loren with her huge eyes and black mane the color of a shiny piano; Sophia Loren smiling flirtatiously at the camera with her shoulders uncovered; Sophia Loren in her film *Marriage Italian Style*, Sophia Loren smiling in front of her mansion in Rome, Sophia Loren in torn clothes beside Peter O'Toole in *The Man of La Mancha*; a full-body shot of Sophia Loren, with those exquisite curves of her waist, her thighs, her calves, her arms, her buttocks…

"What are you doing in here, asshole?" My mother appeared suddenly in the doorway of the closet and I jumped; what shocked me more than her unexpected arrival was the fact that never before had she addressed me with a word of that caliber.

"Nothing, mama," I felt naked and humiliated, "I was just looking at all the pretty pictures you've got here…"

"Get out of here right now!" she screamed, blustering like a raging bull. "You have no right to go through my things! I can't believe that you've done this to me! I didn't raise you this way! You've betrayed me! You've humiliated your own mother! You've destroyed everything I ever taught you! But you'll regret it! You'll regret this for the rest of your life!"

"Mama, I didn't want…"

Completely beside herself, she leapt on top of me and clawed the photos out of my hand, and in the same moment she stumbled and fell flat on her face. She tried to keep herself from falling by grabbing hold of the clothes hanging in the closet, but simply collapsed in a heap with coats and all. My mother on the floor! My first reaction was to help her up, but she was so enraged and upset that she refused my offers violently, pushing my arm away and punching me in the face in the process, making it quite clear that she neither wanted nor needed my help. "Get out! Get out of here!" she screamed with all the force of her lungs, while I backed away and saw her as she really always had been: a lone battler against the world who on this occasion had been knocked out of the fight by her own son.

What happened next was so painful that I can barely recall it. She took one of her favorite dresses, tore it at the waste and ripped it to shreds. She then began to wipe her face with the strips, crying helplessly in shrieks and sobs, cursing the world and disowning me, hurling a barrage of insults whose rage and frustration I couldn't possibly reproduce on the written page. She then turned the closet light off with a slap of her hand, and crawled towards her bed, sobbing and saying that nobody had ever hurt her like this before, screaming with mounting wrath that the crime of my insolence would weigh upon me for the rest of my existence, and that my tiny brain was not capable of understanding what I had done. "You foul sack of shit," was the last thing she said to me.

For me, this scene was truly unbearable. I felt as if the Brooklyn Bridge had collapsed on top of me with the full weight of its iron cables. I was mortally flattened; my mind had crumbled in confusion and despair. My vision went cloudy and I leaned against the wall to keep from falling over. Finally, I staggered from her room like a man on death row, feeling culpable for every vile act ever committed, from the crucifixion of Christ and the atrocities of Hitler to the emotional collapse and physical degradation of the person I loved and admired most from the bruised bottom of my stupid heart.

10

AFTER THAT INCIDENT, nothing was ever the same again. My mother enclosed herself in a wolfish sullenness, following a routine that filled the hours and isolated her from any conversation. She woke up early to say her morning prayers, left breakfast on the table for me and went to work; then she came home at night and went to her studio to paint until she collapsed into her bed. The number of visitors diminished notably. She gave me her attention whenever it was strictly necessary; she checked my grades, prepared my sandwiches for lunch, gave me money for the bus, and looked after me when I was sick. But I sensed, in spite of her attentions, that I was no longer the center of her life. She, nevertheless, continued to be the center of mine.

It was at this stage of my life, as might be expected, that I came into contact with drugs and psychoanalysis. They were two very different territories, of course, but both were equally murky, and both formed an indissoluble part of the cultural atmosphere of New York City at the end of the eighties. Drugs were, among other things, the main common link for the youth of my generation. They were taken at parties, in the street, at home and at school. They were a basic ingredient of that chaotic constellation of brotherhoods that swarmed around the city. Any member of any street clan knew that drugs provided a sense of belonging to the group and a certain position within the hierarchy. Cocaine conferred status. If it was of high quality it was expensive and could only be obtained in small quantities, but the tiniest pinch of that white dust had the power to convert a hopeless loser into the leader of the pack, the king of the barrio, the superhero of the Bronx or Queens. Anyone could gain access to this compensation for existence for a hundred dollars... a price that placed it well out of my reach.

Marijuana, on the other hand, was common currency. It could be obtained on any street corner in the neighborhood, and it had become as popular as tobacco. My friends smoked it to relax, and as a result I always saw them in a state of peace that resembled be-atitude. I remember clearly the first day that I slipped into that il-licit world. It was dawn, and Samantha and I had left an apartment in the Village where there had been much talk of painting and the constant drone of Charlie Parker's sax as if it were a mantra. I had been as bored there as an animal in captivity. Shortly before saying goodbye, one of Samantha's friends offered us a satchel of pot as if it were the most appropriate baggage for the return jour-ney. And in fact it was, because before boarding the subway on the way home, a small sampling of that spiritual herb was enough to inspire us to contemplate the daybreak on one of the historic benches in Washington Square, and we sat looking in wonder at the colors that streaked the sky. Wow, I had never before seen such beauty; the clouds were impregnated with a Mexican rose pink that looked like a fire in the distance, and the white marble arch was illuminated as if it were the threshold to an imaginary kingdom. What an incredible show! If this is what drugs were (I thought in that moment), if their effects could bring you to a state of enlightenment that could make you forget the miseries of this world, I was ready to become their most fervent devotee.

Samantha did not appear inclined to share this ecstatic and contemplative vision, which seemed to me unusual for a woman who loves painting so much. She appeared to be immersed in a state of extreme anxiety; she looked around in all directions as if she were being harassed by an army of watchmen, and she did not find a moment's calm, not even when I dared to caress her cheek. Unfortunately for me, we were not on the same wavelength. "Let's go!" she said to me in a voice that seemed to emerge from the caverns of panic, and in the middle of that dawn of fire, much against my will, we set off on the listless homeward journey to Brooklyn.

On the subway, the panorama changed completely. At that time of day, in the empty cars of the first trains, we were able to sit down face to face. I found myself enveloped in a profound drowsiness brought on by the warm underground air, and the sound of the movement of the train along the tracks drilled into my eardrums. The world seemed to move much more slowly when I turned my head towards the window and stared at the graffiti scrawled on the walls of the subway car, and returning my gaze towards Samantha I observed her carefully while my face welled up with an absurd pressure, on the verge of a hysterical explosion. Her face seemed to me the funniest thing on Earth, and I burst out in a loud guffaw. She broke out simultaneously in deafening laughter, and the world turned into a playground of unbounded hilarity, a roller coaster of mirth that slid onward without brakes from station to station.

It was all very strange, because while we laughed at our own laughter time froze as if by magic. When we got off the train at Brooklyn Station (close to my house) the sun was on the rise, although it could not have been later than seven in the morning. As we were hungry, we went into the first open restaurant that we came across for a hamburger, and while we chewed the cobbled meat we recalled our laughter and returned once again to that senseless joy that made us accomplices in banality on the run together from our sound judgment.

Of course, after the period of drug-induced apotheosis comes the crepuscular moment of fatigue, when you head off to bed, weighed down by defeat, to recover the lost energy. But this was not the case for us; at that time we were overflowing with adrenalin. We ran through the streets hand in hand like the fugitives we really were, and on entering my house we didn't even check for the presence of my mother. Luckily, she had just left for work minutes before, which allowed us to relax in the living room undisturbed. Then we climbed the stairs lethargically to lie back on my bed like two weighty bundles pulled down by gravity. Everything seemed to be happening naturally and spontaneously. So naturally and spontaneously that I decided to take a shower in front of Samantha. Well, not exactly; I simply wanted her near me. So I led her to the bathroom beside my mother's bedroom, sat her down on the stool beside the sink and slowly began to strip off my clothes. When I was completely naked I lifted her chin to my lips and kissed her sweetly, with calculated slowness, serene and joyful. Her lips opened up with a concealed longing and I touched her lightly on the cheeks with the exaltation of knowing I was naked in front of someone totally dressed, but who had the spark of desire flickering underneath her clothes. Mmm, my skin began to burn like a lit torch, my member grew pointing towards her body, and then I left her and stepped into the shower as if nothing had happened. After a few seconds I soaped up my face and touched my penis, feeling it as firm as a sword, and in the midst of the rushing water I felt her put her hand over mine. Yeesss, I lowered my hand gently and she took hold of me sweetly, and then I felt her breasts against my back, her stomach against my buttocks, her lips on my neck, her body like a small guitar that hugged me as no woman had ever hugged me before, and the hair of her pubes rising and falling against my lower thigh while she hugged me masturbating herself with my body and me with her fingers. Ahhh, this was just what I needed, an incandescent carnal encounter, and I turned around to hug her and to feel her chest against mine, to press her stomach against me, to feel her legs wrap around mine, to breathe in unison, to pass the tips of my fingers through that virgin yet at the same time familiar territory, until our breathing accelerated and our desire began to seek an improvised form of release, something out of the norm and utterly democratic.

It was then that I understood that sex moves the world. As the hormonal excitement increased we left the shower without turning off the boiling torrent of water, we caressed and kissed each others' soapy bodies with an eagerness uncontained, we crossed the threshold of the bedroom banging against the walls, I felt her soapy belly against my unsheathed virility, she groaned and sunk her tongue into every part of my body, desiring her deflowering with a warlike vehemence unknown even to her, and then I took her by the waist and lifted her onto my mother's bed, I looked into her face, and felt ecstatic at the sight of the beauty of her huge eyes, her thick, trembling eyelashes, her smile that welcomed me like a ship coming into port, and that gentle yearning that gave way wildly to an incomprehensible emotional whirlwind in which Samantha delivered herself to me with vulva open to swallow me as if it were the immense mouth of a serpent, while her arms wrapped around my neck and my helpless throat felt the inevitable weight of asphyxiation, my beloved friend transformed into an octopus with tentacles that strangled me with the force of a Cyclops and the breath was crushed out of me while desire yielded to shock and my virility constrained itself and my eyes grew wide with fear and my mother appeared demanding her quota of power and cut off my sex while laughing hysterically and ordering absolute submission to each and every one of her brutish intentions.

I can't express it in words, but in that incipient moment a terrifying force took hold of me that shook my drug-numbed body and shredded what capacity for comprehension I had left in my brain. Then I saw in a flash of prescience that my lover had transformed into a many-headed dragon, my mother's bed burst into flames while my eyes sizzled in boiling oil, and while Samantha was ready to give herself over to an uninhibited and profane plea-sure, I was suddenly consumed by a supernatural terror that drove me to leap from the bed and run naked down the stairs and out into the back garden in a sudden fit of humiliation, as if the mas-ter of the house had just come in to discover me interrupting the daily routine and unrivalled tedium of a hopelessly unhappy and bored housewife.

11

PSYCHOANALYSIS WAS, FOR me, an even more debilitating experience than drugs. To begin with, not only did my mother not believe in such practices, but she was almost totally ignorant of them. And I, as a devotee of all my mother's beliefs and prejudices, hardly felt inclined to explore them. Samantha, on the other hand, had various friends and relatives who were immersed in the mysterious studies of the unconscious, and believed firmly that intensive therapy (three sessions a week) would help me overcome certain inhibitions. It wasn't that Samantha had suddenly begun to acknowledge that I had flaws; she continued to believe that in some part of my brain there existed that ingredient of genius that she alone had discerned in my offhand remarks, and that sooner or later my talent would bloom naturally; she was nevertheless convinced that all human beings (even overachievers like myself) hauled around a heavy burden that, if they developed into neuroses, could hold us back irremediably from the realization of our full potential.

Needless to say, it was Samantha who presented me to her psychoanalyst uncle, and who took responsibility (without saying a word to me about it) for his fee.

He was a very cordial man, of course, but the sessions with him seemed to me the most futile and tedious of experiences. I would arrive at a small house in the vicinity of the Lincoln Center, furnished with rustic wooden objects and paintings of European landscapes, and this gentleman would ask me to pass through to his office, where I would have to lie down on his couch and start blathering about the past and present events of my life. To me it seemed that none of what I talked about was interesting; to him, everything I said was highly significant and definitive.

Psychoanalytical theory is based on the rather daring and outrageous principle that nobody in this life acts out of conscious motives. What we do for love, for self-interest, for money, for fun or simply for pleasure, is actually in obedience to other motivations (none of them at all admirable, incidentally), which are kept hidden in the cellar of the unconscious. Applying this theory to my life, the great revelation was that everything I did or left undone revolved around the pleasures or displeasures of my mother. All my acts sought her approval, while my omissions sought to prevent her fury. What a revelation! After various interminable sessions of rummaging around in my past, the conclusion was a diagnosis that to me was blatantly obvious.

On this journey through the dark recesses of my unconscious, my doctor (as he called himself) introduced into my life two characters utterly strange to me and, furthermore, totally alien to my character and personality: Oedipus and Henry Miller. The first isn't worth elaborating on much; some time ago a certain Freud had arrived at the demented conclusion that all men desire their mothers and are, potentially, their fathers' assassins. When my doctor spoke to me about this, identifying it with my situation, I thought his astute analysis to be nothing more than a bit of leg-pulling. But to humor him I went out in search of the book *Oedipus Rex*, a Greek tragedy so popular that it could be found in any bookstore in Manhattan. I read it in a single sitting. I had never so much as perused a work of Classical antiquity, and its plot struck me as totally bizarre; poor Oedipus was doomed by a brutal and senseless prophecy, and he proved incapable of freeing himself from his fatal destiny; he was doomed to kill his father and sleep with his mother. To add injury to insult, the unhappy devil punished himself for his crime by gouging out his own eyes. Sounds logical? Even the names of the characters in the story seemed to have emerged from the delirium of a lunatic: Jocasta, Laius, Creon, Tiresias. What the hell did all this have to do with me?

Nevertheless, psychoanalysts are committed to proving their ludicrous ideas by whatever means necessary. The doctor knew (he got the truth out of me in an unguarded moment) that Samantha and I had been naked on my mother's bed and that in the climactic moment of our encounter I had run from the room, overcome by an incomprehensible terror. He felt this sufficient to drill me with his theory of my profound dependence on my mother, my hidden sexual desires for her, and the metaphysical horror that drove me to possess her. And then, to top it all, he offered me the example of Henry Miller, a writer whose work oozed sexuality. According to my psychoanalyst, I should follow his example.

How? By way of an emotional purging that would liberate me from my own mother, a conscious recognition of my repressed attachment to her, a liberation from my state of infantile vulnerability, and a radical severance from my subjection to her desires, her whims, her fears and her reproaches. Furthermore, the doctor proposed that I, just like Miller (who had also done his time in hell in Brooklyn) should abandon New York and go far away, as far away as possible, to Paris. I should follow his example and devote myself to what I really enjoyed: traveling, studying, meeting people, breaking my own boundaries, listening to music, reading, writing, releasing my own suffering onto the page, perhaps writing a novel over the powerful influence of my mother. Sheer nonsense, in other words.

12

WHETHER PROVOKED BY the drugs or the psychoanalysis I don't know, but there began to appear in my dreams an intimidating and recurring delirium: I dreamed that I was living locked up in a medieval dungeon, sometimes chained to the damp and foul-smelling walls, or bound to the bars of the window through which I could view the outside world. Inside, everything was squalid, gloomy, deathly. But outside, as far as I could manage to see when I peered out through the bars, was a field of flowers extending towards a cliff. And beyond was the sea.

I didn't fully realize it, but an irrepressible desire for freedom had begun to plague my addled brain. I wanted to go, to get out of the barrio, to see other towns. There were afternoons when I left the magazine store early and took off for Manhattan racing like a lunatic, crossing the Brooklyn Bridge at full speed, sensing the bridge's suspending girders beneath the soles of my feet, taking in the profiles of the buildings at twilight, until I reached the vicinity of City Hall, exhausted. Then I would wander around the buildings of the old port, passing by the fish markets and stores on the docks, and lingering for hours to watch the boats docking and banging over the waves, imagining myself on board, sailing to other continents.

On one of these aimless expeditions, after meandering through the bustling streets of China Town and Little Italy, I was walking around the Village like many of the students who go there in search of their own mantra, and, after spending endless hours on the edges of the jazz clubs and chess halls (knowing that I was forbidden from those privileged circles where the intellectual elite would gather), I decided to take Fifth Avenue up towards Central Park, and when I got to Madison Square Park I sat down on a bench to contemplate the stars of the winter evening above that historical part of Old Manhattan. Right in front of me was the Flatiron (at the beginning of the twentieth century the tallest building in the world) in all its majesty. God, I loved that building! Its antique bearing, its triangular profile, its frontal blade parting the avenues seemed to me the ultimate product of the steel-framed architecture that should never have succumbed to the unrelenting pressure of Art Deco and the mirror skyscrapers that reflected the aspirations of the future. And then, in the blink of an eye, I saw him. He was one man among the millions of ordinary pedestrians swarming about the residential districts of southern Manhattan, but he had that proverbial magnetism that radiated from his unmistakable figure on the silver screen. Robert De Niro, talking on a street corner. I was stupefied. It was him, the loony taxi driver who accumulated a diabolical arsenal to protect a teenage prostitute and to challenge the world with his ballistic strategies; the young and dashing godfather Vito Corleone, who took advantage of the fleeting opportunity offered by a parade in lower Manhattan to shoot at point-blank range at one of the self-proclaimed kings of the neighborhood and then went home with a shiny apple for his son; De Niro, the overweight boxer who gained God knows how many pounds to play the part of heavyweight champion Jack LaMotta; De Niro, the noble missionary who defended the Brazilian natives against their own government's unjust war of extermination. De Niro, the hero with charisma in spades; the villain of unbridled cruelty; the leading man who takes away the breath of every woman in the world; the idealist Mafioso, the simple martyr. Robert De Niro, the figure at the top of the very short list of men I admire in this life.

Seeing him in front of me, just a few yards away, I underwent a kind of existential metamorphosis, for want of a better name. It was nothing otherworldly; I did not experience a mystical awakening or a humbling epiphany that opened up my eyes to the transcendental truth that in the ordinariness of life and the reality of the street, we are all equals. No, what I felt was exactly the opposite: far from seeing the mythical actor as a normal human being, I felt as if I was acting in a movie. Reality itself had been transformed. It was no longer tangible and concrete, to put it simply; with De Niro there, in the middle of the street, the real world had been converted suddenly into an illusory vision, an image on celluloid. De Niro was at the center of everything, protagonist of a secret, mysterious plot. Those of us around him were the extras, the ignorant masses, who in spite of our marginal status were participating in and helping to shape an epic tale. The world was invested with purpose and meaning. We were all part of a screenplay conceived by someone else. God existed from that moment: life itself was the most convincing argument for His infinite creativity. It didn't matter that most of the actors didn't have the script. By being a part of this monumental work, each one had an original and exclusive role to play in the cast. The only thing we had to do, in accordance with the instructions, was to act conscientiously upon that amalgam of latent impulses inside us that we have given the name of liberty.

De Niro had his hair slicked back to reveal a high forehead (the vestiges of that superb personification of Al Capone that he had just played in *The Untouchables*) and he was smoking and laughing with his sarcastic grimaces while listening to a large and robust black man with bulging eyes and a proud display of teeth, speaking in the vociferous style of Louis Armstrong, with an overcoat draped over his large frame. It was cold, but the days of snow had not yet begun. What was curious was that people were passing by without seeing them, just like in the movies, and as I analyzed them calmly and closely from the opposite sidewalk, it truly looked like one of the more emotive scenes from *Once Upon a Time in America*. De Niro was listening with scattered attention to his interlocutor and smoking anxiously, until suddenly he pointed a dartlike finger at the broad chest of the other man, and took his arm, directing him to walk. Together they began marching westward down 23rd Street in the midst of an ocean of heads emerging from offices at rush hour and making for the subway stations.

Automatically, as if obeying the instructions of a hypnotist, I began trailing them at a distance. I took care not to be seen, like a detective following his target. I was still the clandestine cameo star in an unreleased movie. I walked behind them without losing sight of them for a second; it had become my life's mission. In this investigation, I was engraving in my memory a collection of data that might prove useful to me in the future: De Niro wore a beige gabardine jacket that swayed with his gait, and he brought his heel down forcefully with each step, just like one of those stockbrokers who considered themselves the lords of the South side. He was wearing a pair of those Boston shoes that he had consecrated in his role of the gangster. Occasionally he turned and looked behind him, as if he suspected I was following.

What were they talking about? It was impossible to know. Serious matters, no doubt, because there was no laughter exchanged between them. From a distance, it didn't look like a relaxed meeting between two friends. I followed them for several blocks until they stopped in front of the entrance to the Chelsea Hotel. For a moment, I thought that my investigation was to stop there, that they would go up to one of the hotel rooms to discuss movie matters. I felt lost: was on the point of being written out of the essential screenplay of my life. I would end up on the cutting floor. But no: De Niro and the other man merely paused in front of the hotel and then continued walking towards the Hudson, and before arriving at Eighth Avenue they went into a café where I was able to observe them from behind a newspaper stand: they sat down face to face, beside the window that looked out onto the street, like in the movies. I felt like the cameraman. All that was missing was the soundtrack of their conversation.

De Niro had taken control of the discussion. He had stopped smoking so much, and had managed to stop up the verbal outpour of his companion. He was speaking with a persuasive force capable of intimidating anyone. It wasn't that the other man was meek, but everybody knows that De Niro's majesty is not easily matched. Much less in Manhattan. De Niro spoke, emphasizing each phrase with his hands, and his argument appeared as convincing and conclusive as a pistol to the chest. Just like *The Godfather.*

While I carried out my modest role of spectator on the opposite sidewalk, a few yards from the window where Robert De Niro spoke to his companion, explaining some Quixotic hypothesis with arguments that compelled him to put his greatest dramatic skills to use, there appeared on the scene the sporadic silhouette of a rather attractive woman, around forty years old but with a well-preserved, slim and shapely figure, who stood in front of De Niro with an alluring air, as if challenging him to give an immediate answer to some request made earlier. This added a new freshness to the scene. The sight was so natural that I thought at first it might be an untimely admirer. But it wasn't. It was someone who fulfilled her particular role with assurance, a new character who had studied her part in the film to perfection, and who had made her appearance in a calculated way at the exact moment when the plot called for it. I took a good look; I liked her attitude, and at first I didn't recognize her. I simply accepted her inclusion in the scene willingly because she added an ingredient of feminine smoothness when she interrupted the tensest moment of the conversation with such calm boldness. But a few more seconds were enough for me to observe her outline more carefully and recognize in her a set of familiar features that began ringing bells in my head. Then, as if I were in some Arabian hall where the veils of the dancer were falling and revealing an increasingly familiar reality, I made out the unmistakable profile of my own mother. My mother, in a scene with Robert De Niro. My mother? I felt a sudden jolt, a shock similar to a club to the head.

"May I ask what you are doing standing here?" A voice ringing with authority spoke into my ear. I was so absorbed in the cinematographic vision that the voice sounded to me like a distant echo, although its owner was right by my side and his presence was sufficiently imposing for me to decide it appropriate to overlook the impertinence of his question.

"Nothing, officer. I'm just watching Robert De Niro."

"Robert De Niro? Hmmm, and do you always spy on stars like this before asking for their autographs? Hmmm... look, boy, don't try to pull my leg. Look at who you're talking to. You're not talking to Mel Brooks here, you get me? You'd better come with me, because your attitude is very, and I mean very suspicious."

"No!" I cried at the top of my lungs, pointing to De Niro, and in the instant that the officer turned his surprised face towards the window of the café where my mother was disappearing from the scene like a ghost, I took off down the sidewalk and recklessly leapt across the busy street, narrowly avoiding a shattered hip offered by a car passing by at full speed; I ran to the opposite sidewalk and dodged the crowds as I fled for Seventh Avenue, while the police officer chased after me shouting incoherent remarks from the other side of the road, panting and making all kinds of wild gesticulations with his colossal figure and his three hundred pounds of rage, sweat and adrenaline.

In those days I was an agile youth (those were the days!) and I could fly like a bat out of hell without even catching my breath. In a short space of time, barely seconds, I had managed to execute a series of acrobatic jumps that allowed me to change route and outwit any pursuer. One! I slip into the crowd on the sidewalk. Two! I leap over a crate full of vegetables. Three! I take off like a bullet past flower stands, garbage cans, news and magazine counters, the people jostling around the subway entrance, hot dog carts, doormen in their livery, lost tourists looking for Soho and cars swerving out of my path to add an element of traffic hazard to the chase, and in my frantic escape I hear a persistent murmur inside my head, telling me that if I stop I'm dead, like the unfortunate black man who had confronted the police completely openly because he was innocent, and had to pay with his life for the simplistically dualistic outlook of a mentally challenged white guy in a uniform who could only make sense of the world by dividing it neatly into good guys and bad guys. And in the mad chase, I actually felt like one of the bad guys, as if I had actually committed a crime, and as I ran off the set of the movie with De Niro, his outspoken companion, my mother and the hundreds of extras who moved like robots around the central scene of my life, I felt as if I'd been expelled from that paradise of the living where conflict doesn't really exist, because the good guys are never at odds with the authorities or with other good guys.

After crossing Fashion Avenue without even acknowledging the oncoming cars whose drivers berated me with their honking horns, I looked back to see the distance that separated me from the outraged policeman. Noting that he had fallen behind between the florist and hotdog stands, I changed sidewalks again to lose him, crouching down after sliding over the hood of a vintage Studebaker and slinking like a shadow towards the doors of a church.

Ahh! A sensation of protection, of seclusion, of safety suddenly enveloped me. This abrupt change of atmosphere is what best defines the architecture of a temple: inside, the atmosphere around you is transformed, turning silent and dark, and the light that filters in through the stained-glass windows is so tenuous that it resembles the first rays of daybreak. There, amidst the columns that support the arches of the vestibule, every pore soaks up the air of religious reverence, and in spite of the fact that I had come to this sacred place with my soul aflame with fear and agitation, my presence in this sanctuary produced in me the same devotion felt by the most ardent of churchgoers, those who come to pray and sing and to feel themselves a part of the human race.

A mass was underway inside. When I came in, I leaned up against the wall and then slipped instinctively into one of the rows of the faithful who prayed on their knees with their hands together. I imitated them even while I threw a glance back to see if the police officer had come in, and, identifying nothing suspicious, I lowered my head onto my hands as I knelt, in a humble gesture, giving thanks to heaven for having helped me escape from the justice of men, which with each passing day seemed to me more earthly and devious.

13

THE NEXT DAY, my mother was in a much dourer mood than usual. She deflected any question that might distract her from her private worries while she bustled round the living room dusting off her collection of porcelain dolls, pushing the vacuum cleaner over the cloth of the sofas and the rug, cleaning out every corner and cornice with an obsessive burst of energy as she ensured that her domain was utterly free of dust, disorder, or the subtle effects of passing time.

"Mama", I said tentatively, "do you know Robert De Niro?"

My mother stopped her activity for a moment, as if my question had caught her off guard. Then she resumed the task of wiping the ashtrays on the living-room table with her cloth as if nothing had happened.

"Yes," she answered without hiding her irritation, "I've seen him in a few movies... not all of them good, by the way."

It was obvious that she did not want to discuss the matter. In fact, she did not want to talk at all. Automatically, as she tended to do on such occasions, she raised a protective wall between herself and the world outside with her silence, and as always, she made me feel like an intruder who insolently sought to violate the last bastion of her privacy. Nevertheless, I armed myself with sufficient valor so as not to be defeated by her first reaction, and with a firmer tone, I told her:

"I saw you. It was yesterday afternoon. You were in a café on 23rd Street, near the Hotel Chelsea. It was you, I know it was. And you were with Robert De Niro."

"Have you gone nuts?" She suspended her cleaning frenzy and shot me a lightning bolt look of fury. At once I felt a shiver from the base of my spine up to the nape of my neck, but at the same time I was determined not to give up on my first attempt. Then I heard myself say:

"I was on the sidewalk across the street from the café. It was Robert De Niro. I know because I followed him for several blocks. He was with a black guy who looked like a heavyweight, the two were arguing heatedly... and there you were. I know perfectly well that it was you. In the beginning I didn't recognize you because you had your hair tied back, but then I saw you clearly. You went up to De Niro and..."

In that instant I was compelled to suspend my allegation. My mother turned on her heels, took a step towards the sideboard where her porcelain dolls sat, bent down with a swift movement, took from the sideboard the figure of an eighteenth century Florentine nobleman and hurled it at my face with all her might.

"You asshole!" she screamed with a fury that sounded like it had been accumulating over years, and in the midst of my confusion I raised my arms instinctively to protect myself from the projectile just at the moment that the porcelain figure was soaring towards my forehead. My quick parry saved me from a collision that would have mercilessly cracked my head open; thanks to my lightning reflexes I avoided a trip to the hospital to contain the hemorrhage and sew up the wound with a row of stitches above the eyebrow.

"How dare you follow me?! So now you're spying on me?!"

Completely out of her head in a fit of extraordinary and disproportionate rage, my mother started hurling the porcelain dolls at me, and then the china plates, the ashtrays on the table and finally even a small copper pot that she had brought from Michoacán, but all with such bad aim (luckily) that the only thing she succeeded in doing was to smash all of her decorative pieces against the wall behind me, and shatter the glass of the only painting hanging on the wall. Finally, in a rapture of impotence and aggression, she leapt at me like a Nordic warrior, with a determination and ferocity worthy of a she-wolf defending her young: the paradox of the scene was that the invader this mother wolf was lunging at was her own cub.

In that critical moment, I was perfectly composed; now I realize that something inside me had changed. Instead of being intimidated with fear (which was my habitual response), I put into practice the few lessons in self-defense I had taken, and when she threw herself on top of me I used her own impetus to launch her, with a simple movement of my arms, towards the main sofa in the living room, where she sank into a momentary confusion at discovering my abilities in the martial arts. She would never have imagined that I would stand up to her like this. Nevertheless, far from admitting defeat, she jumped at my neck with feline elasticity; but instead of strangling me, she began hitting my chest with closed fists, like someone trying to knock down a closed door bolted in several places, quite aware that her efforts were in vain. In this position, it was not difficult to hold her down, and I squeezed her against my chest to contain her rage.

Gradually, she began to calm down as she realized that she had been overpowered. At first, on realizing that she was restrained in my embrace, she shook her head with canine fury, clenched her teeth and muttered blasphemous syllables and lycanthropic growls. But soon her rage began to lose its impetus, as her efforts to free herself proved useless against the straightjacket hold I had on her.

"Easy, mama... easy. It's all over now... easy."

I then experienced in real life one of those scenes that appear so often on movie and TV screens, where some woman bursts into a rage of titanic proportions, taking a kitchen knife and transforming into a killer, capable of castrating the heavyweight wrestler who lives next door or destroying every movable object in her house in record time, only then to descend into an inconsolable and cathartic weeping that releases her tension in rhythmic movements and allows her to return to a normal state with her spirit purified. In the moment that my mother gave in to the resilience of my stranglehold, she entered into a kind of emotional withdrawal with a heavy sigh, her chest began to vibrate as if in a prelude to weeping, she lowered her arms slowly in gradual capitulation, buried her face into my chest in search of refuge, and started to sob with an emotion that rose up from the darkest depths of her battered soul. I calmed her, cautiously releasing my grip and stroking her head while she gave herself up utterly to her tears. For the first time in my life, I saw her vulnerable and vanquished, defeated by her own exertion and subject to a force superior to her own, which in this particular case happened to be mine. At that moment, I felt imbued with a power until then unknown; I saw myself as captain at the helm of our family, the authority figure who imposed his will by force, and while she fell to pieces mumbling intermittent phrases and holding me with something resembling tenderness, I felt my manhood awaken slowly; I became aware of the size of her breasts against my chest and my heart gave a jump. But as my mother seemed to be so comfortable with our closeness, I gradually let go of my shame and entered a state of completeness akin to Buddhist enlightenment; the space around me became warm and inhabitable and the world at last seemed to be my own, a home to which I had the right for the simple and natural fact of having been born.

14

THE FOLLOWING MORNING, just as we had agreed the night before, I met my mother at the café where I had seen her chatting with Robert De Niro. The south side, on 23rd Street, a short distance away from the Chelsea Hotel. It was quite an elegant place, with wooden tables and chairs with elaborate designs *a la francais.* There were Toulouse-Lautrec prints on the walls and a long bar at the back, and the clientele was diverse enough to include groups of college students and middle-aged women frittering away their mornings discussing the hottest tidbits from *Cosmopolitan.* There were also a few solitary customers unraveling the misery of their existence at the bottom of their coffee cups, and the occasional bright star of stage or screen, like Mr. De Niro.

My mother was one of the waitresses in this establishment. Just like the others, she wore a uniform consisting of a long blue skirt and a black vest over a white blouse, with a red kerchief around the neck. *Tres francaise.* She looked stunning, and when she saw me, she came to the door and welcomed me as if she were the hostess. As I had guessed she would, she led to me the table next to the window looking out onto the street, and offered me the chair where De Niro had been sitting the day before. I took my seat while she continued carrying out the role she played daily, and as I perused the menu I saw, passing by on the opposite sidewalk, the police officer who had pursued me so bitterly some forty-eight hours earlier. I was not afraid; in fact, I looked directly at him with seriousness and disdain, like someone catching sight of an enemy whom he had vanquished in the past, whose memory had been erased with the passage of time. And in any case, I was busy taking in the spectacle of my mother, whom I had never seen working outside the house before. She was like she always was: in a whir of constant activity, attentive to every detail, diligently attending to her customers' needs, assuring that nothing was lacking at the tables in her care, removing finished plates at once, urging the cooks to deliver the dishes more promptly and offering each of the diners a smile, as if she'd never been happier. And yet, she was different, because for the first time I saw her as an independent being, separate from me, a woman whose object of primary concern was no longer her son. I believe that on that morning I saw her as she really was; neither more nor less. She was no longer a goddess to me. She was simply a Mexican waitress in one of Manhattan's hundreds of restaurants, a workingwoman who had made it on her own, raising her son through sacrifice and self-denial, and now feeling herself freed of a burden that had perhaps been too heavy for too many years.

"Do you need anything?" she asked me when she took away my espresso cup. "If there's anything you need, anything at all, just let me know. That's why I'm here. I treat all my customers the same, but you I'll treat better than De Niro."

"As a matter of fact, there *is* something I need, mama," I answered with my newly acquired confidence, "I need to make it up to you for everything you've done for me. It may seem weird to you, but I hate to see you working all day. You've worked enough. You've paid off a house. You got me through school. You fed us both. You've done enough."

"Hey, hey, hey, don't forget that I'm your mother..."

"That's just it, mama." I took her by the hand and made her sit down at my table. "I think it's time you had a rest... and I want to tell you something that I've been thinking about for some time... I want to go back to Mexico. I want to study there. I want to go back to where I came from. I want to see my country. I don't know exactly when, but I'm going. And I'll send you money from there. In our family, the money wiring will be going in the opposite direction; I'll send you money *from* Mexico. So you don't have to work so hard. And I'm going to get a degree. Maybe I'll study postgrad in Europe. And then I'll send you pesetas, francs, pounds, deutschmarks. So you can stop working. Wouldn't you like that? I know you would. I know you, and I know that deep down there are things that you like doing apart from working. You love painting, for instance. And you like writing, I've realized."

My mother had her eyes cast down to the floor, and was listening in silence. Had I ever seen her listening in silence before? Yes, but not to me. It was an honor she paid almost exclusively to Señor Miranda. She didn't generally listen to me; she simply gave me orders. She answered my questions, of course. She was a model mother; but nothing more than that. She was also a woman who, as a general rule, did not listen to what others had to say. She paid attention only to what interested her, and her comprehension had a kind of filter that denied passage to any superfluous clutter. All the information she received was carefully screened. Suppose, for example, that she heard a talk about Jane Fonda, who in those days was one of her role models. If Jane spoke of how she kept her perfect figure as the years went by, or of the series of marriages she'd had, or of the movies she'd made, such information was dismissed out of hand. But if she spoke of how she'd managed to become a luminary in so many fields, or of the sufferings she'd had to endure, or of the effort she'd made in her performances or of the political ideas she professed, that information not only became engraved in my mother's memory but also constituted an object of study for future inquiries. It had taken me long enough to realize it, but my mother had a keen interest in politics. An unusual interest for a waitress, perhaps, but my mother was a most unusual woman.

"Haven't you noticed that I've grown up?" For the first time I looked her up and down.

"Of course I've noticed," she answered without the slightest trace of irony in her voice, although the remark might well have been a *double entente*, because by that time I had grown to outmeasure her by three inches.

"I'm not a kid anymore, mama... and I know that this is going to hurt, but I'm not *your* kid anymore..." (now she was the one who did not dare to look me in the eyes) "...and you owe it to me to treat me like an adult. You can't hide things from me anymore, mama. I'm not a kid who can't think or decide things for himself... I know exactly what my possibilities are, what my limitations are, and..." – here my mouth went too dry to continue speaking – "what your limitations are..."

Instead of getting angry, and without raising her eyes, my mother smiled with an air of mischief. She pressed her lips together to avoid ejecting an impulsive word, and after a few seconds she lifted her gaze and looked at me with... how can I describe it? A strange mixture of affection, curiosity, satisfaction and... a certain respect. Perhaps, in her heart of hearts, she had realized that with my new attitude I was closing a cycle, fulfilling a mission that had begun when we first arrived, without a cent, on that island of immigrants' hopes that was Manhattan, the heart of the world.

As for me, sitting in that chair where my idol had sat just the day before, I felt big, powerful, capable... owner of that unshakeable self-assurance that was the property of Robert De Niro.

15

THE NEXT DAY, steeled by the strength that standing up to my mother like a man had given me, I went in search of Samantha. Although I hadn't seen her for several weeks, I didn't feel the slightest hint of remorse. The chapter of our sexual misadventure was, in my opinion, definitively closed. What remained open (or at least so I thought while I sought her out in the lofts of her friends in the Village) was that unique quality of establishing a metaphysical connection, sharing our daily pleasures and displeasures, vibrating at the same emotional frequency, conversing and listening to each other attentively, dancing that dance in which we invented new and unknown moves and at the same time rigorously followed the classic steps as if we had learned them from years of disciplined practice in a dancehall.

I can't deny that I admired her, and that, more than anything, I was profoundly dependent on the admiration that she conferred upon me so arbitrarily, by chance or in confusion.

In that moment, hoping to find her on some corner of Bleecker Street, one of the feelings that truly overwhelmed me was an enormous, immeasurable sensation of power. I remember walking down the streets of New York with my shoulders back as if I were the owner of the thousands of tons of steel in Manhattan.

I felt not only powerful, but truly invincible. It was a wonderful feeling. Having fearlessly stood up to my mother's hot-tempered fury, my confidence in my own judgment had been boosted significantly. I had left my childhood far behind me. I had grown up, extraordinarily, in a matter of minutes. And as an adult, I radiated an immeasurable potential. I knew it all. I understood it all. And what was more: I could do it all.

On a corner of Washington Square, I picked up a lead on Samantha. She was not in the Village. Her cultural preferences had shifted to other neighborhoods of Manhattan, they told me. She was no longer into jazz, blues, or the silky voice of Ella Fitzgerald. Much less the hollow thrills of drugs or the fantasies of literature. Samantha had returned to her first love, that passion that made her walk this world believing herself to be among the chosen: figure-skating. Knowing the simplicity of her *weltanschauung*, I took off without a second thought for the place that was one of the proverbial cathedrals of ice-skating: the rink at the Rockefeller Center.

Which was where I found her.

As always, there were more than a hundred people on the ice, from couples skating hand in hand to mothers with their small children, all dressed in mittens and woolly hats to protect them from the cold. And *Samantha* was the queen of the rink. She skated at a dizzying speed, with perfect cadence, moving her arms rhythmically to increase her velocity, gracefully evading the other skaters on the rink, and doing spins, jumps and pirouettes with a style and finesse that attracted the attention not only of the others on the ice, but also of passers-by. She hadn't seen me, which permitted me to watch her safely from the anonymity of the crowd.

It was obvious that I longed to be with her, to walk through museums and gardens at her side, to resume our inexhaustible conversations, to feel the electric spark from her glance, to hear her spur me on calling 'Chase me, *Javelin!*' in the midst of our games and, above all, to touch her, to feel the tenseness of that flesh that called to me like never before to run my fingers over its smoothness and enter into that carnal and sacred communion where instinct guides us and solitude disappears... and yet, the moment allowed me to open a parenthesis, to refrain from calling to her and watch her in silence, and thus I remained, following her routine without missing a detail while she went twirling backwards with all the grace of her figure, and used the empty spaces on the rink to execute stunning jumps and turns. On one curve, she arched her back and raised her arms as if ready to take off in flight, the blades of her skates in line as if on tracks, toes apart and her whole body like a leaf trembling in the wind, while she inclined her head over her shoulder and smiled, knowing that she possessed an elegance and levity shared only by skaters and seagulls. Then she bent down again into attack position to pick up speed, pushing herself forward with that force of the thighs that ignited my desire, and she turned her body round to prepare for her back flip, and in the moment of changing direction she took off twirling into the air with her arms firm against her chest, making two complete turns before touching down on the ice with her arms raised in a gesture of triumph.

Then I decided to follow her, and I went forward to the edge of the rink to rent some skates. It wasn't so full, and although I was an inexpert skater I stepped onto the rink spurred on by the novelty of having an encounter with her on ice. I hesitated for some time at first on the edge of that great frozen rectangle, holding firmly onto the wooden barrier as I tentatively tested my abilities on the skates. Then I ventured out a few steps, with enough impetus to slide furtively as I pushed myself forward with my feet pointed diagonally, digging the blades into the ice with increasing self-assurance, until I got to the curve and tried to cross the right foot over the left to make the turn, but with such poor coordination that the back of my right blade got jammed into the front of the left, and I lost my precarious balance and dove headfirst at the feet of the statue of Prometheus while the other skaters dodged about me and eyed me with either commiseration or mockery.

And *Samantha*? When I got back to my feet I looked around for her. The rink had emptied out a little and she was there in the center spinning like a top, squatting with the left leg stretched out in front of her while she held herself up firmly with the right skate and turned round at a vertiginous speed. There was a crowd watching her, and some applauded as if they were watching a professional show. I moved towards her. The front of my pants and shirt were soaked from my fall, but my unshakeable self-confidence had rendered me impervious to shame or fear of ridicule. Surely she would look at me with delighted surprise and laugh, praise my daring for having come onto the rink without knowing the most elementary rules of skating, and take my hand and haul me across the ice at ever greater speeds to challenge me like she always did.

But there were so many people between us, and my clumsiness increased exponentially when I attempted to dodge the other skaters. I had still not reached the middle of the rink when Samantha resumed her usual rhythm and sailed off to the outer edge of the rink at high speed. Suddenly, when by chance a child slid into her path, she pulled up forcefully, bending her ankles and digging the blades in like spades, raising a spray of ice flecks that surrounded her and magnified the beauty of her style. She continued on at her unmatchable speed, but I was determined and I started following her around the rink from the inside, close to the center, where I worked on my turns and built up my speed with more success than before. I followed her like this from my advantageous position on each lap of the rink, and had managed to avoid sliding or falling for a reasonable time, until at last I decided to catch up with her at the end of the rink near the sidewalk where the passers-by gathered to watch, right in front of the flags that confirm the universality of the Rockefeller Center.

Calculating her speed so as to intercept her at the midway point of her trajectory, I set off quickly with the toes of my skates pointing outwards, as my instincts dictated, and as I advanced, a lady with a child who was skating with a level of skill similar to my own suffered the misfortune of getting in my way just as I came to within a few yards of the boardwalk at the end of the rink, and in an effort to avoid knocking the child down I grabbed at the lady's waist so that she fell onto my lap as we hit the ice. The child, left standing safe and sound, began to cry, while I slid out of control towards the boards with his mother on top of me.

Remarkably, this second fall did not diminish my enthusiasm at all. The lady I had knocked over with my momentum was furious, but finally accepted my apologies (after all, her kid was fine) and once the incident was over I went in search of Samantha, to catch up with her at all costs. And then, suddenly... my resolve abandoned me completely.

In the middle of the crowd, I saw Samantha again. She was taking flight, raising her shoulders and moving her arms rhythmically, but accompanying her skilful display was an additional pair of skates. There were no longer two skates making fabulous figure-eights in front of the enormous Christmas tree, but four; four legs moving in unison to the music of a nonexistent waltz, and four arms waving rhythmically on each turn, pushing forward and embracing each other to create a style that united them inexorably in every movement.

I suppose the show must have been extraordinary, because the people on the rink had deferred to the presence of this pair of professionals, and had gradually given up their places as skaters to become spectators. Samantha and her companion had captured the attention of everyone, and when at the end of several peremptory turns (which they had no doubt practiced countless times) they took over the center of the rink and closed their performance with a spectacular spin that looked to me like something from a circus show (he lifted her by the waist while she raised her arms like dove's wings) and the audience applauded furiously. Finally, in a revealing moment that dissipated any of my lingering doubts, she kissed him on the mouth.

It was a kiss without the slightest hint of passion, as cold as the ice below their feet. But it was clearly a kiss that suggested a relationship beyond mere professionalism. Unavoidably, as happens in the course of nearly all biographies, Samantha had found her mate. It was clear enough just from looking at her brimming with happiness. I was standing only a few yards away from them, and just when I expected it least, Samantha noticed me in the crowd and waved at me to come to her side. I turned my head as if I didn't know her, and left the rink in the opposite direction.

PART TWO

1

I LEFT NEW York to escape Samantha's ghost. Her memory chased me through the streets, hounded me in the bookstores and cafés, sat down beside me at my desk at school, and cornered me in my bed at night. Some friends told me that this is always the way with the first love; that her memory takes root like an alien body buried under your skin, and it cannot be extracted until another alien body finally displaces it.

In my case, the second alien body never showed up. Or if it did, it didn't have the strength to displace the first.

I went to Mexico City with the aim of obtaining a degree in my country of origin. My mother knew that this would happen sooner or later, and without offering any resistance she did all she could to help me on my way. She rearranged my bedroom to make my absence more endurable, she gave me the details of some friends and contacts she had in the Mexican capital, and she bid me farewell without a tear in her eye. She assumed her role like a professional. She also sent me money to defray the costs of my studies, at least until I found a job as an English-Spanish translator for a movie magazine and began giving private English classes.

I rented a small apartment on the street Calle Medicina, right next to the university campus, which meant I could get to my classes by merely crossing the college thoroughfare. I enrolled in a degree program in International Relations, because to begin with I wanted to make sense of the relationship, so close and so contradictory, that existed between Mexico and the United States. I soon learned that the subject was much broader than I had expected, that the analysis of relations between the nations of the world requires a precise theory and methodology, and that the pressures of globalization were expanding the parameters of study at the same rate that they were reducing the size of the world.

Without really knowing where my diligent attitude came from, I threw myself totally into my studies. Nothing mattered more to me than statistical analysis, international trade, multilateral treaties, the global economy, public and private international law, or the comparison of political systems. I devoured the works of Quincy Wright, Samuel Huntington and Octavio Ianni. I became an expert on all the agents of international relations: the State, foreign policy, diplomacy, international government departments, multinational corporations, the United Nations. All my conversations revolved around these topics. As did my friendships. I chose my friends from among the most outstanding students, and my relationships with them consisted in determining who had the greater knowledge of each subject.

We were living in a time of great upheavals. The Berlin Wall had been pulled down and broken into thousands of tiny pieces that were being sold in Germany as souvenirs. The Soviet Union, the socialist fatherland in the world, had disintegrated into the many nations that had been patched together after the invasions of the Tsars and the 1917 revolution, and the geography of the world was changing at a dizzying pace. In my classes they spoke of a new world order, and we, as students, burned the midnight oil in interminable discussions to find the best way forward for a new international reality that seemed to us beset with chaos and turbulence. And after all, who was going to save the world if we didn't?

In those days of youthful megalomania, barriers didn't exist. We formed study circles, discussed documents, proclaimed our ideas all over the campus, drafted manifestos, sent letters to newspapers, debated hotly, clung fiercely to our causes, and tried to disseminate our beliefs by any means available. We were intolerant and sectarian, and we had no patience for error. The truth was a collective, immobile commodity. Anyone who crossed the line drawn by the group was expelled for good.

Unlike many others, I was not afraid of isolation. Having grown accustomed to hanging around on my own in my childhood, exclusion from the group did not worry me at all, and I never considered it a punishment for my criticisms, my doubts or my ideological independence. On the contrary, I viewed my solitude as a kind of aura that set me apart from the crowd and reinforced me in my convictions. And this attitude, which now seems to me the height of arrogance and pretentiousness, served in those days as a powerful magnet of female admiration, a shiny bait at which all kinds of fish came to bite.

My small apartment was just big enough to fit my bed, a few bookcases, my desk, a kitchen table, a record player, a kitchenette and a bathroom. It was not, by any means, the ideal location for student gatherings. It nevertheless served this function, particularly for female students, who would often arrive in bunches for my evening discussion meetings. They would take up positions on the few chairs available or on the floor and read and discuss theories until after midnight. The direction of the debates dictated which of these young women would demonstrate the argumentative skills necessary to stay on to talk with me. The Socratic dialectic filtered out the less able. Gradually, those dismissed went back to from where they'd come, slinking down the stairs with scarcely a goodbye, until the one who was the most well-versed in the topics of discussion sat before me, challenging me to defend my points of view against hers, opening the last beer in my refrigerator, and, after a brief verbal skirmish, leaping on top of me to initiate another type of battle, knowing that the night was short and that we would have to reach the heights of pleasure before daybreak and the resumption of classes.

My relations with women were pretty cynical in those days. I believed that in Mexico City there was a more or less fluid sexual exchange similar to what existed in New York – after all, both were cities with cosmopolitan atmospheres and huge populations – where everyone chose their partner at random for a single night, and on the following morning the lifestyle of the individual imposed its own restrictions. Pairs would part with a hurried kiss, and lose each other in the anonymity of streets and offices. Then, at the end of the day (if they still had the appetite) they would have to begin again from zero on a new hunt for fresh flesh. But in fact, there were no similarities. What happened in Mexico was something very different. To begin with – although it was not obvious – women considered sex a kind of intimate branding, an indelible mark that declared their preference for the male and demanded continuity in the relationship, something that could not end when the two participants in the coupling dressed and parted to carry out their respective daytime activities. In other words, they didn't sleep with just anyone. Of course, for men (or at least, for me) this detail was not at all clear, and as it was never explicit, I didn't worry about keeping up appearances with the kind of farewells that were considered appropriate. I never said anything like "now I know you better I like you more", and certainly nothing like "you are mine and I don't want you to be with anyone else". This incited considerable frustration and numerous bitter reprisals from women who told me, for example, "you are as cold as your fucking ideas"; or epitaphs like those of one young woman who shouted in my face "I don't give a shit about you and don't even dream that I'd ever come back here" just because I had woken her up and told her to leave because I couldn't concentrate on my studies with her intermittent snoring.

There was one girl, named Graciela, who seemed to be extremely superficial, but who displayed a wit that suggested something beyond mere sarcasm. We therefore saw each other more often than was my custom. After a while, I discovered that she was in fact quite sharp and astute. One day, she began trying to give me a lesson in good manners, and ended up hitting upon exactly what was wrong with me. She was a drama student who combined her acting classes with a course in diplomacy, and she had the perfect face to play a witch. In children's plays, she was always given the role most appropriate to her physiognomy. This didn't seem to bother her; in fact, she seemed to enjoy these performances hugely. She was a little sadistic, perhaps... in any case, one day at my place we'd had more than a few drinks (tequila, beer, tequila, beer, tequila...) and while we were making love she raised herself up high and then dropped, and extended her arms with desperation as if she wanted to scratch something into the walls, and after we wrapped each other up in an animal embrace, with fingernails digging into my back and panther growls, she sat up in the bed and began to beat me on the chest, furiously, as if she wanted to smash me apart or absolve sins that had nothing to do with me, and perhaps nothing to do with her either.

"Open up!" she cried in desperation. "Open up!"

Her scream sought to open up my chest. Or something more: it sought to open up my flesh, gut me at the level of my breastbone and pull out my beating heart.

"Why are you so shut up inside?" she said, gritting her teeth and pleading with her eyes. What did they do to you?"

'*What did they do to you?*' That question struck me with its retrospective force.

I didn't know what they had done to me, but I suspected that they had left me without feelings. Or at least, without feelings that I could handle in the way I handled my ideas. I had built an

insurmountable wall to defend myself from the outside world...
To forget something that hurt me like a thorn buried in the darkest corners of my subconscious... I had put my neurons to work
to assimilate theories and explanations about the concrete reality
of the world: the independence of the Baltic nations, the wave of
democracy that was sweeping over Eastern Europe, the end of the
Cold War... Explaining the international scene, I felt invulnerable.
Nobody could touch me, everything had a rational explanation,
nothing could take me by surprise. Meanwhile, inside me was an
abyss that was growing wider and wider, which nobody, least of all
me myself, could hope to face...

"Take up acting, asshole, because if you don't express what
you've got inside somehow, you're going to die." Graciela gave me
a savage slap on the chest with the palm of her hand and burst
into tears.

I lit a cigarette, imperturbable.

2

I am Emilio Montalvo Sanchez.

Does a man's name say something about him? Is there a connection between the personality of the individual and that cluster of syllables that identifies him socially, that affords him legal status, that singles him out in his family, that permits him to go to school, to get a job, to get married, to have offspring, to be checked into a hospital bed, to be recorded in an obituary and to have something engraved on his tombstone?

I am Emilio Montalvo Sanchez.

Until that day, I had not really been conscious of my name. I was my mother's son. She never called me by my name. She always called me "*hijo*", son, or when she was in an affectionate mood, she called me "*m'hijito*", my little son. "*Hijo*, come here." "*Hijo*, put your coat on, it's getting cold." "*Hijo*, I don't want you to do that again." When she was with other people and she spoke of me, she always told them: "my son can take care of that", or "my son will go with me." And come to think of it, that generic identity was reciprocal, because I never called her by her name either. She was always my mama. Thanks, mama. Yes, mama, I understand what you're telling me. No, mama; I won't be late. I never said to her: "Julieta, I'm home," much less: "I don't like how you treat me, Julieta."

My friends gave me a series of nicknames, always with short words that identified me in a group of classmates or neighbors. The most persistent sobriquet I was given was at elementary school, where they called me "Mex", because I was, in the beginning, the only Mexican in the class. The teachers, worn out from struggling with dozens of children from New York City's lower classes, never used our names. They addressed us by pointing with a finger: "You, the second chair", while those more inclined towards camaraderie would say simply: "Hey, buddy."

I am Emilio Montalvo Sanchez.

That name didn't mean much to me when I graduated with honors after completing a thesis on the seasonal migration of Mexicans to the United States, a well documented analysis of the needs of various American hotels for cheap labor to take care of the cleaning and kitchen work that American workers were not willing to do, which was therefore assumed by migrants from central Mexico. The commentaries from the faculty heads were all highly complimentary, but few friends heard them. My mother could not come down from New York for my graduation, and I didn't organize any kind of celebration to recognize the event. It was nothing more than a technical step that allowed me to obtain a scholarship from Mexico's National Council of Science and Technology to go and study in Paris; I never framed my university diploma, nor did I ever sign my letters as "Mr. Emilio Montalvo Sanchez, B.A. Hons."

"*Je m'appelle* Emilio Montalvo Sanchez," I said without conviction to the man in front of me.

"No," he told me firmly, "*I* am Emilio Montalvo Sanchez."

The fact that he answered me in Spanish, after I had caught up with him at the corner of Boulevard Saint-Michel and la Rue des Ecoles, sent me reeling back into the past. I had been studying for nearly two years at the Institute of Economic and Social Studies in the Sorbonne, and my days were taken up with lectures on texts about identity and conflict, crisis management, the culture of peace, confrontational geopolitics, international human rights, multilateral war solutions and the treatment of refugees. In my free time, I snooped around the bookshops in the Barrio Latino, read in cafes, and watched movies from all over the world. I had a Peruvian friend with whom I had made the pact to speak in French so that we could practice as much as possible and mutually correct each other's errors (or rather, so that I could constantly correct his pronunciation), and I had just recently begun sharing an apartment with a French woman. I had integrated myself fully into student life in Paris. So to hear Spanish suddenly, and from a man who introduced himself with my name, threw me unavoidably back into my past; to a past that I had succeeded in forgetting completely.

"Look, wait a moment," – the man foraged around in an inner pocket of his coat for his wallet, from which he removed his passport – "... here's my identification. My name is Emilio Montalvo Sanchez."

The situation could not have been more confusing, annoying or absurd. I basically lived from the scholarship that I received from Mexico, and, as was my monthly custom, I had come to collect my check from the bursar's window in Mexico House, in Paris' Latino quarter. In nearly two years, I had never had any problem claiming my check. But on this disconcerting and (as I discovered later) providential occasion, the check had already been claimed when I got there. How was it possible? The young lady who attended me at the window told me that the person had identified himself correctly, and when I showed her my identification with my name she just shrugged her shoulders and said: "if there are two people with that name, it's not my fault."

I asked her for the most detailed description possible of the person who had picked up my check, and once I had one (a pretty vague one, incidentally, apart from his height and the color of his clothes), I ran out to the street to chase after him. Some students talking on the corner of Rue Saint Jacques told me that they had seen a person fitting the description headed for Boulevard Saint Michel, and thanks to my swift feet I caught up with him in the vicinity of the Musée de Cluny.

"Pardon, Monsieur..." I said, catching my breath, *"... vous avez mon cheque... Je m'appelle Emilio Montalvo Sanchez."*

His response in Spanish left me breathless. And his identification left no room for doubt. And yet... was it not possible that he was an impostor, someone who had been trailing me to discover my name and financial situation, falsify my passport and thus deprive me of my monthly income?

"No, look," I showed him my student i.d., "I'm Emilio Montalvo Sanchez... There's been a mix-up... you must have collected the wrong check... The check you've collected is a scholarship from the Mexican Council of Science and Technology..."

"I have a scholarship from the Mexican Council of Science and Technology," he replied with a composure that began to exasperate me. In that moment of bewilderment, gasping from the chase and stunned by the absurdity of the situation, I felt that my own identity was detaching itself from me as if in a dream... I did not know whether I was mistaken, if in reality there was another check for me, perhaps made out to another name, or whether the man in front of me was taking his performance too far and was making fun of me...

"That check is mine! Give it to me!" I took him by the lapels of his jacket and began to shake him. Although he was slightly taller than I was, I was sure that I could quickly defeat him, but the moment he saw that he was being attacked he delivered a strong punch to my sternum that doubled me over in pain. This was not at all a French response, because the French would never resort to fisticuffs so quickly. The man was clearly Latino. You could tell from the color of his skin and the hardness in his eyes, quite apart from his fluency in Spanish. Having freed himself from my grip with his fierce strike, he left it at that and walked off quickly, but I was far from defeated... I caught up with him near Boulevard Saint German, in front of a boutique, and I took him by the arm and threw a punch that connected with his cheekbone so that he staggered a moment. Then I realized that he was carrying a portfolio, which fell open to the ground sending folders and papers scattering all over the sidewalk. I leapt at the papers in the hope of finding my check among them, and in the moment that I bent down I received a kick in the face that split open my eyebrow so that I began bleeding profusely. By this point, people passing by our scuffle began showing their indignation, some shouting insults as they passed, supposing us to be a pair of belligerent Arabs. I stood up with bloodstains on my shirt-sleeves and managed to deliver a punch to his stomach before he seized me by the neck, forced me down to the ground and pressed me against the asphalt. I saw him above me with his face twisted in rage, but I could tell that something was holding him back; he could have asphyxiated me there and then because nobody seemed inclined to intervene in our fight. Before the sound of the first police whistle he had already left me there on the ground, picked up his portfolio and scattered papers, straightened up and tucked in his torn shirt, and, after spitting on the ground as if to declare the conclusion of our dispute, he dashed away down an alleyway in the direction of the Seine. I gasped for air and staggered to my feet, battered from the scuffle and pushing my way through the crowd that watched me with a mixture of reproach and commiseration for my disgraced condition of the defeated.

Before the police arrived I picked up my belongings, whatever I found there on the ground. I was in physical agony from the fight, and I began weeping with rage, but to avoid the cops I gathered what strength I had left and ran for the Jardin du Luxembourg. There, sitting on a bench to catch my breath, I revised my papers to take stock of what I had lost, and I found that I had picked up his passport... it was a Mexican passport... just like mine... with his photograph... his personal details... and his name... Emilio Montalvo Sanchez.

3

ISABELLE, MY ROOMMATE, was a beautiful woman from Marseilles with large green eyes and an elegant figure, who had grown up and developed intellectually during the long years of the Mitterrand government. I had met her by chance at one of the summer concerts organized on the grounds of the Pompidou Center, and had been seduced by her easy laughter, her childlike enthusiasm, her relentless curiosity and... her singular interest in all things foreign. In a Paris swamped with Arab immigrants and ultra-conservative xenophobes, it was hard for a foreigner to find acceptance among the locals. You could familiarize yourself with all the main streets of Paris, speak French without an accent, identify every dish of French cuisine, but... only French citizenship could give you style, class and grace. For the French, heritage defined the status of the individual. Paris, that axis of the fusion of many cultures, in reality professed an implicit rejection of the barbarians from the world outside. Isabelle's openness to me was therefore an oasis.

"Another person with your name?" she said, pursing her lips and raising an eyebrow in a sign of astonishment. "Forget about it! Coincidences like that are bad omens..."

Professionally speaking, Isabelle was multi-skilled. She had worked in the country crushing grapes in the vineyards, and since arriving in Paris she had been employed as a clothes ironer in a Laundromat, a library assistant, a waitress, a babysitter, a gardener, a baker, a secretary, a clothes store salesperson, a photographer, a receptionist and a model. She was only a little older than I was (she was 31 when I met her) but she seemed to have lived several lives. Her most stable job had been working as an assistant to Danielle Mitterrand in the management of her international affairs, when the grand Madame unexpectedly decided to support the guerrilla cause of Subcomandante Marcos in the jungles of southern Mexico. This awoke in Isabelle a sudden interest in all things Mexican: its geography and history, the mythical figure of Emiliano Zapata, jungle vegetation, the country's indigenous groups and Mexicans in general. It was at that moment that we met.

"Don't give this guy too much importance..." Isabelle began casually singing *Alouette, gentile Alouette, Alouette, je te plumerai.* "There are millions of people with the same name in the world..."

I had been living with Isabelle for a few weeks, and things were not going smoothly. She had a four-year-old daughter, and her maternal behavior was not quite as humanitarian as the principles proclaimed by Madame Mitterrand on her international tours. Overwhelmed by the daily enslavement that the girl represented and by guilt for wanting to be free of her, she screamed and mistreated her constantly. I was no children's rights activist, but the scenes that I witnessed day after day exasperated me. I usually held my tongue and brooded over an uneasiness that I drowned in my reading. When I did intervene on the girl's behalf, things got substantially worse.

The fact that I had found a compatriot with the exact same name did not fit into Isabelle's strategic plans for Mexico. My chance encounter did not involve indigenous people, or Latin American folklore, or the exposed sores of underdevelopment, or human rights violations. The loss of the check interested her, of course, representing as it did a significant blow to our struggling economy. But all the rest, such as the circumstances of the encounter, my existentialist doubts, the open curiosity and unusual level of importance that I gave to my own name after the incident, were of no interest to her at all. So when one morning I tried to distract her attention with the subject of the other Emilio in the middle of a ferocious reprimanding of her daughter, she was overcome by a fit of proverbial impulsiveness and blurted out furiously:

"You've spent weeks on that topic, *salaud!*" She looked at me with eyes like daggers. "If the guy with your name bothers you so much, go and live with him!"

I got the hint, if that is what it was. With little regret, I went and packed my bags.

4

AFTER QUESTIONING VARIOUS friends and acquaintances and looking up telephone numbers for the surname, it finally occurred to me to check in the records at the Sorbonne. And there it was. There I was, of course – student in Economic and Social Development, and the address that until a few hours earlier I had shared with Isabelle – but he was there too. Emilio Montalvo Sanchez, student in Information and Communications, member of the Aztec Dance Workshop, 1 Rue Victor Cousin, 75 230 Paris, telephone number 01 40 46 25 48.

"Hallo?" a male voice answered at the other end of the line.

"Does Emilio Montalvo live there?" I asked tentatively in Spanish.

"Yes, he does. But he's not here now. He's at work..." The accent did not sound Mexican.

"Ah, excuse me. Look... I have a document of his that I would like to return to him..." I said, a little apprehensively. "Would you be able to give me his work address?"

"Yes, of course. You know how his workplace is always changing, isn't it? But right now he is working in the north of the city... somewhere around La Villette, but wait a moment... the exact address is the corner of Rue du Maroc and Rue de Flandre..."

That was close to the Riquet Metro station. I got on at Saint Michel station, changed at Gare de l'Est and traveled from there to Riquet. On the way I got to thinking, and then began to suffer from that sense of time spoken of by one of Julio Cortazar's unforgettable characters, a man with the ability to relive long periods of his life in the few minutes it took to get from one Metro station to the next. Who was this individual with the exact same name as mine? Of course, people with the same name do exist, Isabelle was right; there are the dozens of kings with the same name, the two Napoleon Bonapartes and the thousands of John Smiths, of course, but to have the same given names and the same surnames was not an everyday phenomenon. And we were also both Mexicans, surely – there was no National Council of Science and Technology handing out scholarships in any other country – we both spoke Spanish and we were both studying in Paris. Isn't it surprising? We were also both good fighters...

Coming out of Riquet station, I emerged onto Rue de Flandre and walked in the direction of Rue de Mardoc. When I reached the intersection, I began looking around for something that might be his place of work. I checked in the places that offered the greatest possibility of finding him: a bakery, a grocery store... there was no office in any of the blocks abutting the corner concerned. Finally, I found him on a medium-sized construction site just a few yards from the intersection. There he was, the young man with whom I had exchanged blows for our misunderstanding over a check, unrecognizable in his work attire. He was dressed according to his station; a pair of grey overalls that hung on him loosely, a flannel shirt with red and blue squares, a pair of hiking boots that looked tough enough for any task, and a hardhat for protection against falling objects. Under the hardhat, a bandana covered the back of his neck. They seemed to be building something like a theater or an open-air parking lot, and the man was in the midst of demolition work, breaking up rocks of average size with a sledgehammer that he swung from his back to the ground with a ferocious force that made him groan with the effort.

I moved towards him cautiously, and at a close distance I could see he was sweating like a Viking. I took note of the muscular tone of his arms, and in that moment I gave thanks to heaven for not having to fight with him again. He, meanwhile, appeared to have shut out the outside world completely. He was concentrating exclusively on his work, and all that consumed his attention was the stone in front of him. "Aaaaahhhh!" he roared as he raised the hammer and let it fall with a crash on the rock. "Aaaaahhh!" he cried when inertia compelled him to renew the attack. He looked worn out from the exertion, but something inside him made him continue in spite of his exhaustion. "Aaaaahhh!" In his trance, he could not be distracted, and so when I called to him with a certain hesitation he showed no sign of having heard. He had barely finished breaking one rock when he raised the sledgehammer back above his head and let fly with another forceful strike. Once in a while, he stooped down to collect a pile of rectangular blocks that would be used to replace the floor that he was breaking with his blows, and when he lifted them I saw his biceps grow to the size of grapefruits with the effort.

I moved closer uncertainly. When he saw me he shaded his eyes with one hand and squinted, as if he had difficulty focusing on my image.

"I've come to apologize," I said looking at him directly in the eyes, "I didn't know that there were two people with the same name in the Sorbonne... I checked it out and I found out that there were two checks, both written out to the same name, but to different people..."

The man stood looking at me without saying a word, gradually recognizing me, carefully measuring my words and movements.

"And also," I took his passport out of my jacket pocket and held it out to him, "I picked this up in the street, and I wanted to give it back to you..."

"Ah!" his face lit up with surprise. "I've been looking for it for days... thanks."

In that instant, just when the other Emilio gave a hint of a grateful smile that seemed an acceptance of my hopeful attempt to break the ice, there arrived hastily onto the scene a man dressed in an old suit (it was immediately clear that he was not a construction worker) with the air of a foreman, who as he approached blurted out in a French laden with a Russian accent: "What's wrong with you, Emilio? Not time for chat! It time for work!! Understand me? Time for work! W-o-r-k!! Work!!"

His aggressiveness got my blood boiling. It seemed a propitious occasion to make use of the knowledge I'd just recently acquired from my master's course in international labor laws.

"Look, Mr...." (the intruder didn't take my pause as a hint to insert his surname here) "...we know that these are working hours, but that doesn't give you the right to shout at any worker like that. Do you understand?" The intruder eyed me with a seemingly anthropological curiosity. "No... I can see that you don't understand. You are committing an offence, sir, because according the most recent amendment to the Workers' Code, in the article referring to work conditions for foreign workers, the directors, administrators, foremen and other employees representing management are not permitted to undermine the dignity of their foreign workers, under penalty of a fine and the withdrawal of their license. Do you understand now, sir?" The intruder appeared stunned by my defense. "What is important for you to understand, and I am telling you this for your own benefit, is that if you persist in your attitude, the person who is going to lose his job is you... yes, sir! You! Do you understand me, friend? Look..." I showed him my Sorbonne student identification. "I'm a field researcher for a student research team, studying work conditions for foreigners. Get the idea? And *you* are going to be our case study... and with that attitude of yours, our research is going to be a success, because we're looking for examples of mistreatment of foreign workers.

You are going to be famous, my friend... but you're also going to to in some big legal trouble..."

The intruder did not wish to continue listening to my allegation. He made an annoyed expression, raised his hands to the level of his face with the palms open, and lowered them again as if he was throwing something away, tossing me to the void or ridding himself of some bothersome burden... then, he turned round and left, privately cursing the world.

The other Emilio looked at me for some time with an expression of gratitude, and to avoid further interruptions to his work we said goodbye, agreeing to meet up at the Café de Flore, on Saint-German-des-Pres, two days later.

5

THE WHOLE OF Paris can be found in the Café de Flore. Few places have a history as far-reaching or as weighty, as at its tables have sat writers, philosophers, journalists, painters, actors, movie directors, politicians and tourists of every kind. It had enjoyed more than a century of life, from *la Belle Epoque* up to those controversial years of European unification. I was not a very regular customer (the dishes were out of my price range) but the waitress who served me coffee or wine at the corner table from where the whole premises could be observed always recognized me when I came in. She was a generally good-humored lady advanced in years, one of those typically conventional French women who are part of the furniture in certain upper-class Parisian establishments.

When I arrived, she conducted me with the utmost cordiality to my favorite table. I was lucky, because the place was packed to the gills. It was approaching six o'clock in the evening, and above the restaurant's columns and arches was reflected the dull light of sunset. The place was filled with university students stretching out their academic chats over a bottle of wine, pairs of lovers sharing carpaccio and salad as a gastronomic prelude to a night of passion between the sheets, and elderly people devoting their twilight years and the pleasant resignation of old age to reading...

I decided, in totally French style, that the only thing to do was to share the death throes of the afternoon with a good wine, and I ordered a bottle of Medoc and a small platter of assorted cheeses.

The other Emilio arrived a few minutes later, dressed in the student's attire that he had been wearing the first time I saw him, and he apologized politely in French for being late.

"It's a relief to speak in Spanish with someone," I told him, to establish the language of our conversation from the beginning.

"What do you want from me?" My guest skipped the usual niceties and went straight to the point.

"Nothing in particular," I answered him honestly, "...it's simple curiosity. I've never met anybody, not even in Mexico City, as big as it is, that has exactly the same name as me."

"You're from Mexico City?" he brightened up after pouring himself a glass of wine.

"Yes... well, no... actually, I lived all of my childhood in New York, but I was born in Mexico City, yes... although I don't remember it... I arrived in New York when I was two... I lived there until I was eighteen... then I went to study at the National University of Mexico, where I got my scholarship to come to study at the Sorbonne. I have a scholarship, which is why I went to pick up my check that day and... well, *that* happened..."

I hadn't spoken much, but my throat had gone dry. I poured myself some more wine and took a large gulp. Why was I telling all this to a stranger? Although I knew that he was my countryman because of the confusion with the checks, he had not yet even told me that he was Mexican. For a moment, I felt profoundly stupid and vulnerable. The man sitting before me watched me with a degree of attention disproportionate to the platitudes I was babbling, and in a fraction of a second I recalled the image of Graciela, the girl with the golden curls and witch's face... "Open up!" she had told me. "Open up, you asshole!" So... there I was, opening myself up like a ripe oyster in front of a stranger, in whose face I could not decipher whether my story was of the slightest interest.

"I'm from Campeche," he said in a voice so serious that it sounded like a personal confession, "and I lived there all my life, first in the huts of my village, then in the state capital, and later in Mexico City, just like you... I came to Paris with the money my uncle loaned me, and I've survived here anyway I can...'

"Yes, yes," I said, hoping to guess what he was trying to get at, "Paris is kind of like a dream for humanities students in Mexico, and I guess in all of Latin America. Haven't you heard that saying, "one day I'll get to walk along the Champs Elysees?" A lot of people have the mythical image of Paris from the postcards, Victor Hugo's novels, the movies, the smell of the perfumes, the clichés about how the streets are paved with *haute couture*, but... oh! To study in Paris is something else... it's a hard city, with difficult people, a lot of racism..."

"Hmmm," Emilio served himself another glass of wine. "Do you remember the day you attacked me over the business with the check? There were a lot of people on that corner, remember? And all those people were shocked by the scene, the scandal in the street had shaken them out of their daily routines, they were suddenly witnesses to an incident that belonged in the third world, and so they assumed the fight was between two Arabs... did you realize?"

"Of course I realized!" I replied, amused by the recollection, "Most French people can't even tell the difference between an Arab and a Latino!"

For the first time, we laughed out loud.

"Do you see this beard I get the moment I stop shaving? Well, it makes me look Middle Eastern..." softened by the wine, his expression reflected a mixture of sadness and resentment. "And because of that and the dark color of my skin these frogs confuse me with an Arab and look down on me, like they have to assert their superiority..."

"Well, all the cosmopolitan cities have their share of discrimination against migrants, don't they?" I tried to show my solidarity with him while he poured another glass. "In New York they used to call me "Mex", and that nickname always carried an implicit notion of deprecation, because Mexicans there are second or third class citizens, along with the blacks and the Puerto Ricans..."

"But for me it's the same in Mexico City..." he said, after knocking back his glass. "You don't believe me? Ah! Well just ask me where I lived in Mexico City! Don't you know? Nooo, you, how would *you* know... I lived in the churches. That was my first home when I got to the big city, because I had nowhere to live... yes! In the churches! In the church of El Altillo on Avenida Universidad, in the church of the CUC opposite the university campus, and... I'd even hide in the crypts of the cemeteries to sleep, when nobody realized that there was somebody there sleeping with the dead. Not many know it, but there are hundreds of free hotels in Mexico City... the trick is to know how to get in without anybody noticing, and get out the next morning, shameless and casual, so that the people who see you never imagine that you just crashed there for the night. They'll just think you got up early, you went to an early mass, one of your relatives died and you spent the whole night at a vigil, or maybe they'll assume that you're a very holy type who spends his time praying in the temples, you know?"

At this point of the talk, I scarcely noticed that we had drunk a bottle of wine in record time, almost without having touched the cheese. Then we called for some Armagnac.

"I've had a hard time making friends here in Paris," I looked around to the other tables in the restaurant, and noticed that a pair of girls dressed like students were casting glances our way and giggling to each other. "The French are very... rational, to put it nicely. Or racist, to put it precisely. To make friends you first have to engage in an intellectual discussion. I mean... the French first want to know whether you've read Roland Barthes, Michel Foucault and Jacques Derrida, and if you have they put you through an exam on their theories, and if you pass then maybe they'll speak to you again at the next party... but most probably they'd rather just talk to each other..."

"Hey, brother," he interjected with a sudden familiarity that transformed his expression, "why the fuck have you got the same name as me?"

"I..." I shot a sideways glance at the girls who were watching us and laughing amusedly. I couldn't tell if they were flirting or making fun of us. "My father's name was Montalvo... but I never knew him... he died when I was two years old. He lived in Tabasco and... he died of pneumonia. My mother was the one who raised me, alone, in New York. Her name is Julieta Sanchez, and... she never talked much about my father... I think she didn't want to upset me by talking about his death. Anyway, the point is that I never knew him..."

"Shit, man, that's some coincidence," he said as the alcohol he'd imbibed began to cloud his eyes, "my father died in Tabasco too. But he was killed..."

There are some things that you never want to hear. You bear the burden of living day to day for the sake of a few certainties, a few gravitational notions that keep the earth under your feet, that allow you to keep your balance in the universe safe in the knowledge that you will not topple into the abyss, to give you a particular direction and a role to carry out in the grand theater of the world; and if these certainties are put in doubt you will stumble and lose all sense of orientation in your life. Perhaps that is why I diverted my attention from the talk, disconnecting myself from the challenging gaze of my interlocutor and looking towards the French girls two tables away who were laughing openly at us, and without caring how they might interpret it, I smiled at them, raising my glass and toasting them for having given me the best pretext for changing the subject. But Emilio went on regardless, his feet firmly planted in a pool of quicksand that was shocking me into blind drunkenness, showing me the world through a foggy kaleidoscopic lens where the images around me swirled wildly in a tide that made me dizzy with their swaying and submerged me helplessly beneath a swelling confusion.

Then I saw that Emilio was saying something that I couldn't quite make out. He was moving his mouth and from his lips an intermittent and monotonous sound emerged, and amidst the fog I recall clearly that he took a wallet out from a pocket inside his jacket, and from the wallet he pulled out an old photo, from many years ago, which he showed me at first at a distance and then placed right in front of my eyes... he was saying something that I couldn't understand, and I wasn't able to focus my vision sufficiently because the images around me came and went as if they were on a carousel, and with great effort I brought my forearms together on the table and looked clearly at the photo, at a man a little older than him, with wavy black hair and thick eyebrows, large eyes and a crow-like look, large, flaring nostrils and a beard parted in the middle, just like mine.

"His name was Emilio too," was the only thing I heard.

6

WHAT DOES IT feel like to have a father? This question arose out of nowhere, because in my twenty-nine years of life up to that point it had never before occurred to me, and when at last it surfaced like a castaway that the world had long given up searching for, it turned into a tyrannical obsession, an urgent, vital need, a deep call to search for a truth that I carried in each one of the cells of my bones, and that until that moment I had been utterly unaware of.

It is not that I was unconscious of the existence of the father figure in the majority of families, but that the force of inertia that daily life exerts upon us all had got me to accept his absence. In my life, my mother was all. She was my mother, my father, my only family. And my case was not unique, because in New York divorce was more common than marriage, and many of my friends lived only with their mothers. And even in those families where the father hadn't moved to another part of town with a younger woman, as a general rule he would leave for work early and return home only for supper and sleep. As a result, I knew all my friends' mothers, but none of their fathers.

Nevertheless, my case was different. Most children did not live with their fathers, but *they knew* who their fathers were. I didn't. Nor did I know what it was like to have a man around the house, someone like the men I saw in the street, who dressed in suit, who had a beard, who owned an automobile. Someone who would talk to me about his life, his achievements, about the problems he had to face when he was my age. Someone who had played basketball in his childhood, who had made team captain in high school, and who now worked hard running an auto-repair shop in Jersey.

Sometimes, to fill that gap, I would tell myself that my life was much better for his absence. A father was probably even more trouble than a mother, I told myself. Someone with a hoarse voice who gave out orders ceaselessly. An authority on everything, who would monitor my every move. A dispenser of stern warnings and punishments... but at times, I also imagined that a father might be a kind-hearted man, a sympathetic listener, a supplier of retail goods, a giver of gifts and rewards to his offspring...

Who was my father? What was he like? What had he thought of me? What was his life like? What was his death like? Had it hurt him to leave me alone when he died? These questions, which I had never asked consciously before, now pricked at my skin like needles. I recalled the drama of Oedipus, that tragedy that Samantha's psychologist friend had made me read, and I shuddered at the recollection. Perhaps, I *had* killed my father. I'd killed him by forgetting about him, by leaving him to fade into oblivion, by never troubling myself to learn more about who he was. I'd killed him by daring to live my life without him, full of pride, without ever even wondering about where his final resting place was.

And these questions led me to others, which seemed out of place at this stage of my life. What was I doing in Paris? Why had I pursued studies in identity and conflict between nations, migrations, and refugees? Suddenly, my whole academic career appeared to me to be a grand rationalization of my own longings. To find my own true identity, I had researched the atavistic roots of the nations; to resolve my own conflicts, I had analyzed in detail the confrontations between different cultures; to under-stand my own flights to foreign lands, I had immersed myself in the study of international migrations; in acknowledgement of my status as a perpetual refugee in distant lands, I followed the trails of the Bosnian exiles... I was on the way to becoming an expert in international relations and to solving the world's conflicts, but I was still incapable of confronting my own condition as an eternal wanderer, torn from my own roots...

Strangely enough, I had always acted with the greatest as-surance when deciding on my studies. But in that moment, I felt within me a new and somewhat disconcerting impulse, which slowly stripped me of my maniacal obsession with my studies and propelled me in other directions, as if, beneath my protective ar-mor of the brilliant student at the Sorbonne and the implacable defender of his own principles, another person was being born, a man not so tied to his opinions, but much more spontaneous, more open to the awakening of his emotions, and much freer. I began skipping certain classes and attending others. I enrolled in Art History, although it was not part of my doctorate. I took a course in painting. I took to wandering around Paris, ambling along the Seine with no fixed destination. I spent hours examining every corner of Victor Hugo's house, I watched the sunset from the École-Militaire with the Eiffel Tower in the background, and, on occasions, when I wanted to plunge into the intricate laby-rinth of my inner world, I explored the tombs in the Pére Lachaise cemetery, trying to find a clue to decipher the legacy of the dead among the living...

And at the heart of all this was the figure of my father, that image that I had forgotten out of convenience and out of apathy, and that now came to me charged with a vertical force that called me back to my origins, to that past so remote that I had believed it dead and had tried so hard each day to bury.

7

To GET TO the bottom of what I was looking for but did not know where to find, I returned to New York City. I took a charter service from Charles De Gaulle Airport to JFK; a flight that seemed the shortest of my life. I went with a sense of resolve, with a clear idea in my mind. I would wrestle from my mother – literally, *wrestle from her* – the whole truth about my father. I had sent her an email telling her that I would arrive the following week, and that I would call her from the hotel. From the hotel? It seemed more than strange to her that I would not be going straight to her house, but she accepted it when I told her that I was taking a course at NYU for a few days, and that my scholarship was covering my expenses, accommodation and plane ticket. I was lying, of course. I lied about the details throughout the whole trip. I said that I would be staying at the Lexington, but in fact I stayed at a zero-star hotel around Harlem, which was more within my budget.

From the moment I looked out the window of the airplane to see the Manhattan skyline, I felt strange. Arriving in New York is always an overwhelming sensation, the great iron city that opens up to reveal a heart of pure fiber and muscle, a constellation of skyscrapers that welcomes foreigners with open arms, that great magnet that attracts immigrants from the four corners of the planet with an irresistible force. I cannot deny that even I felt the strength of its mystical pull.

But in my heart of hearts there was a voice that kept me aloof, that told me that this city was no longer mine, that the road had forked off and destiny – or that internal force that compelled me to make decisions intuitively – had pushed me down the other track, and that in that moment of my life I was coming to New York as a guest – a special guest – and not as a New Yorker at all.

It was a special occasion, and I organized my stay in a spirit of celebration. It didn't matter to me that my exclusive accommodation was a hotel plagued with lunatics, outcasts and cockroaches, or that my first meal was at one of the proverbial hot-dog stands in Central Park. My true objective was elsewhere, and so on the day of my arrival I made a reservation for two people at the Hotel Plaza's Palm Court, perhaps the most exclusive place for breakfast in Manhattan.

The next day I woke up early, put on the three-piece suit that I used in Paris for very special occasions (start of classes or gala dinners) and I took the Broadway subway to Times Square. From there I changed and went north to Fifth Avenue, and I entered the dining room of the Plaza with the coolness and composure of a man about to close a deal with other business leaders of his level. I sat down at one of the central tables, which provide a view of anyone passing through the lobby, and I ordered a decaf while I waited for my mother.

She didn't keep me waiting long. She arrived with almost Swiss punctuality (she had come all the way from Brooklyn) and when she appeared in the revolving doors I felt a flutter in my chest as I discerned her hair as black and disheveled as the night, her noble *mestizo* woman's profile, and her eyes that still shone as brightly as they had in her youth. And nevertheless... for the first time ever, her attire didn't seem to me altogether appropriate. She was wearing a two-piece cashmere suit that made her look like a school teacher dressed up for a class celebration. She was holding her handbag held firmly over her shoulder like an office girl wary of being robbed on the subway, and wearing those high-heel shoes that were all the rage... in the nineteen-thirties.

However, in spite of her awkward and unfashionable appearance, my mother looked happy to see me, and her enthusiasm grew when she made out from her surroundings the ostentation that accompanied the return of her only son. And then... there occurred what always occurs when people are highly conscious of the social class to which they belong... my mother turned around to look for a moment at the marble columns rising to the roof of the dining room, the tied palms that gave a French touch to the place, the other diners who looked like London bankers sorting out their stocks, and then suddenly her spontaneity was suppressed and she lowered her arms to withhold the hug she had for me, her smile froze as if such an expression was the most appropriate to welcome a son she had not seen in years, and she walked towards me with a caution and pomposity that I had only seen before in movies, in those actresses portraying aristocratic women dissatisfied with the unmanageable paraphernalia of their own lives.

"Hello, mother," I said, thinking simplicity the best approach, and, seeing that she had not the slightest intention of embracing me, I gave her a ceremonial kiss on the cheek and pulled out the chair for her to sit beside me and share the view of the lobby where the guests passed by.

"I see that your studies in France are going well," she said without hiding her satisfaction. "This is one of the most expensive places in New York..."

Years had passed and still she had preserved her beauty and her haughtiness. It was slightly disconcerting to see a Mexican waitress in New York behave as if she were the Princess of Monaco. She had acquired a certain standing, in fact, and she stood as an outstanding example of the reality of the American dream: she was a woman who had come to the Big Apple with nothing but a child in tow, and after two decades of hard work she had managed to put together enough money to buy a good-sized house in Brooklyn and send her son to universities in Mexico and Paris. And now that son, who had depended on her utterly and decisively because of the lack of a father, had come and invited her to dine in one of the most luxurious places in Manhattan...

My mother was not a learned woman, nor had she a great mastery of the language, but she wasn't the slightest bit stupid either. She knew that her son now spoke three languages, that he had flexed his cerebral muscle in the university that was the undisputed home of French Rationalism, but she could not display vulnerability before the intellectual superiority of her own son. So she made fun of my ability to invite her to expensive places, without knowing that I had actually made the trip with practically no resources, and that I was staying in rat-infested lodgings...

"I owe it all to you, mama."

"No, *hijo*," her expression began to soften with a maternal smile, "...actually, you were always very clever since you were little... but very, very clever..."

A waiter arrived with a fruit platter spilling over with papaya, melon, peach, watermelon, kiwi, strawberries, grapes and apples. My mother ordered an assorted plate, and the waiter dumped a mountain of blackberry yoghurt on top of it as if it were a cake. I asked for a simple plate of papaya, as I was much more interested in the conversation than in the breakfast delicacies...

"Ha!" I faked a laugh. "That's the litany of every mother! They all say that they have very clever children."

"Your case was special, because..." she took a bite of the kiwi with delight, and then dabbed at the corner of her mouth with that gesture that all women learn by osmosis, "you were all on your own... you know? Nobody helped you..."

"You mean... without a father?"

"No, no, no. That's not what I mean..." I noticed that she was acting naturally now, enjoying the breakfast more than the talk,

"...I mean that you alone set your own goals, without asking for help from anybody... You were very, but very independent..."

"And what about my father, mama?" I asked her straight out, seizing the opportunity. "Why didn't you ever talk to me about him?"

Click, click. First warning light. As always occurred, no sign of alarm registered on her face. When she heard the question, she had her look fixed on the fork jabbed into the papaya and did not raise her eyes nor show any hint of surprise. However... my question had provoked a mild internal contraction, an almost imperceptible tremor shown only in a flush of her skin and a vein on her neck that protruded slightly as if her circulatory system were rebelling while her face became a stone wall that revealed not the slightest trace of what was simmering behind it.

"I've told you about your father many times..." she lifted her gaze and regained her composure. "But there isn't much to say about the case..."

"The case?" I was outraged by such an unfortunate choice of words. "My father was nothing more than that? A case?"

Click, click. Second red light. My mother detected my anger at once, and stared at me like a feline on the defensive; her eyes opened wider than normal, her ears pricked up, her skin bristled... a shiver ran through my stomach and testicles...

"Your father died very young, he was the age you are now..." her attitude showed an emotional control that seemed the product of training. "It was pneumonia, I've told you... I'd prefer to change the subject, because so many years have passed that..."

"But I don't want to change the subject!" I cannot describe the amazement on her face at my sharp interjection. "All I know is the damn story about the pneumonia!"

In that moment, seeking to regain control of the situation, my mother turned to look at the other diners eating nearby, wiped her mouth again with her napkin and shot me a false and threatening smile...

"In that case it would be better to ask for the check. I'm going to be late..."

"No, mama... wait a minute." I felt my heart begin to gallop frenetically. "I haven't finished... Is it too much to ask you to tell me about my father? How did you meet him? How long were you together? How much did you love him? How did you two...?"

"Listen, *hijo*..." she interrupted me with a voice much firmer and more authoritative. "It's obvious that all your studies have not taught you a thing about the important things in life... Do you forget that I am your mother? Why are you treating me like you were interviewing a stranger? You want me to tell you what we did in bed...?"

"I want you to tell me the truth, mama... that's all."

"The truth is that I have to go." My mother lifted the napkin off her lap and put it on the table.

Slowly, as is the case with any decision that a person makes to turn against the tide of inertia and routine that anaesthetizes any manifestation of vital energy, I withdrew from the inside pocket of my jacket a copy of the photograph that Emilio had shown me in the Café del Flore in Paris, and stretched out my arm until it was under her eyes. My mother took it in both hands, looked at it with a perplexed expression for a few seconds, and when she lifted her gaze I noticed that her face was overflowing with an incandescent combination of rage and despair...

"It's my father, right?" I said, swallowing the pool of saliva in my throat.

"Where the fuck did you get this from?" Her expression was aflame and her face began to deform, as if her forehead were beginning to crack open to let out the lava trapped inside. "What bastard gave it to you?"

"It was my brother, or, to be exact, my half-brother." I was shocked into calmness by the language my mother was using. "I met him in Paris out of pure and simple coincidence. He has the same name as me, he's the son of my father as well, but he has a different mother... and he told me that my father didn't die of pneumonia, he was killed..."

"Shut up, asshole!" she screamed in a voice drowning in pain and resentment. For the first time, she burst into tears – a muted crying with an abundance of sobs and labored breathing. I felt a slipknot around my throat, and I recalled the time when she had cried and hit me and had ultimately come out of it purged of her private hell, embracing me and acknowledging me as a man, and no longer a little boy... I was now expecting that the scene would be repeated, that she would break down in a cathartic weeping that would cleanse her soul and allow her to speak openly of her repressed emotions. But instead, she rose trembling from her chair, came forward to my side as if she were about to lean forward and hug me, and then calmly picked up the bowl of fruit drenched in blackberry yoghurt and emptied its contents over my head before I could stop her, so that when I pushed my chair backwards to protect myself the only thing I achieved was to soak my thighs and knees as well, and as the bowl shattered on the floor I heard the alarmed cry of a woman behind me and the other diners around us stood up, catapulted by the fear that the hysteria might spread; the waiters came running quickly to try to help me, and before leaving the dining room consumed in anger and tears, my mother growled in the hoarsest and most despotic voice that I had ever heard, telling me that I was an ungrateful sack of shit and a worthy son of my bastard father.

PART THREE

1

FINALLY, AFTER MORE than a year of searching for him, I was face to face with him. He was an old *campesino*, a farmer with a forehead furrowed with lines, a drooping moustache peppered with grey, unusually bushy eyebrows, an aquiline nose with a scar that ran from the septum to the left nostril, a firm jaw, and those deep eyes typical of people whose lives are tied to crops and to the land, to the sun and to the rain. He had on his head one of those felt sombreros that country folk only ever take off in bed or in church, and a pair of sandals so worn out that they looked like they had crossed every cornfield in southeast Mexico.

His house was a dwelling typical of the people of the region, the legacy of a culture stretching back centuries and which was consolidated with the expansion of the rural haciendas at the end of the nineteenth century; brick walls arranged in a rectangle of only one floor, with a small plot of land behind it; a front porch and a few glassless windows that opened with wooden shutters; a ridged roof covered with coconut palms to protect it from the sun; the bathroom out the back, and inside a single large room that contained the smoking kitchen stove, the wooden table with the daily bread upon it, a few chairs around the table or against the walls, a trunk that served as a wardrobe and three ramshackle beds that had stoically supported the weight of the years.

"How many years have you lived in this house, Don Melchor?"

"Ooooh... I don't remember the years anymore, no, but I was born here..."

In the township of Tenosique, the sultriest corner of the sultry state of Tabasco, the mosquitoes are brutal. They stalk their prey during the cruelest hours of a summer's day, and when night falls, they charge in murderous swarms, ravaging the skin and filling the heart with the desire to leave and never return. They are the hardest test for the city folk who travel to Tabasco to bask in Nature's glories. Those who pass the mosquito test can go deeper into the fertile plain of the Usumacinta River, cross its vigorous flow and rush off in search of Mayan treasures.

That's where Melchor Ortega lived.

I learned of his existence in the state of Campeche, when I went to visit the town where my half-brother had lived before moving to the state capital. On finishing my doctorate in Paris, I proposed an investigative study into the development projects of the World Bank in the humid tropics of Mexico's southeast, and under this pretext I dedicated myself to seeking out my own roots with the ongoing assistance of my half-brother. Faithful to the Mexican tradition of supporting a family member in everything, he put me in touch with a legion of uncles and aunts, cousins, friends and acquaintances who had known my father in his younger years, and who helped me to better understand the nature of his arboreal personality. I use 'arboreal' in the sense that my father was a tree with many branches. He had many brothers, almost all of them deceased by the time I began my investigations. He also had many women, although this was much more difficult for me to research because my informants knew I was his son and discreetly held their tongues. He also had many jobs, many ideas, and, to a certain extent, many personalities.

Did he have other sons, apart from my brother, who still lived in Paris, and me? I still had not found out. Would the others all be called Emilio, after him? Why did he give all his sons, if there were others, the same name? Was it just for lack of imagination?

My initial impression was that my father was not a stubborn or narrow-minded man. He had not been tied to the land all his life; he had tried out various trades with relative success. By origin he was a livestock farmer, a *campesino*, one of those men who had cleared the jungle to plant pasture, and had managed to earn a good living in the meat trade. He was not at all an educated man, but he had that foggy notion of justice that, like saltpeter, permeates the senses of men born in the tropics, which led him to embark on endeavors quite beyond his chosen field. Among these endeavors, incidentally, was guerrilla warfare. Through some of his friends I learned that my father had been in Guerrero and Sinaloa, that he had first had contact with Genaro Vazquez' guerrilla group and then with the League of September 23, and that in Chetumal he helped organize something resembling the Trotskyite cells that the political activist José Revueltas used to write about. My father, a communist? The more I found out about his history, the more my own surprised me. What was his legacy? What part of his personality could be found in my cellular makeup? I was finally putting together the jigsaw puzzle of my life, picking up each lost piece in a different part of the world. I can now see that I myself appear clearly in the photo that my brother had given me in Paris; the resemblance to my father is astonishing. The first time that I saw this similarity was in the Art-deco mirrors of the Café de Flore in Paris, but the discovery had not surprised me; I had dismissed it as due to the effects of the alcohol we had consumed during our unexpected family reunion.

"This man was the very same one who was shot dead on the riverbank," Melchor Ortega told me when I showed him my father's photo. "I remember very well, it was many years ago, but I heard the gunshots... and... well, I was the one who went out to look and found him was lying there, all bloody and lifeless..."

Don Melchor stopped his tale and stared at me long and hard. God knows what he saw, but my face told him that I was holding in a hotbed of emotions that were struggling to escape somehow, and that his words were going through me like the shots from a firing squad. In every interview, I had always managed to keep absolute control of my feelings, to refrain from showing either happiness or sorrow at any moment, just like a neutral interviewer who keeps his distance from his object of study. But in that moment, I felt that the death of my father strike me for the first time as a personal loss, and the thought that not only had a young and promising life been cut down, but that the killer had deprived me of a father for the rest of my days, made my bile rise to my throat. My reaction was so obvious that Don Melchor himself, this old conservative intoxicated by the splendor of his own stories, had to suspend his tale because the echo of his words was piercing my brain and forcing me to inhale more deeply, as if the more he explained the more difficult breathing became...

"Go on, please, Don Melchor..." I said in a faltering voice. "Do you remember where this man lived?"

"Ahh, as if I could forget," Don Melchor smiled, showing a row of teeth worn out from years of use, "it was in José Antonio's cabin, which isn't there any more, but it was close to the river... not very far from here..."

The man had the key that I'd been looking for, I knew it. I'd known from the moment I heard about him in Campeche. There I'd been told that this country farmer had seen the end of the story, had known my mother and father, but that he was a man very reluctant to share his knowledge. So I began searching for him when I arrived in Villahermosa, I ascertained his whereabouts through his friends and acquaintances, and I announced my arrival through a handful of important people in his life, such as the local mayor, the village priest, the elders of the township. When

I arrived he was waiting for me, but I'd never imagined that he would open up his heart as he was doing with me now...

"Got any more photos?" he asked me somewhat boldly.

"Yes, yes, of course." I took out a pile of photos of my mother at different ages and put them in front of him to select from...

"This woman..." said Don Melchor, his eyes sparkling, "... was much more beautiful when she was young... I knew her well, because she stayed here in my house... She was a student in those days, always making trips and collecting all kinds of leaves and small animals... She loved to walk around the swamps and watch the sunsets and sit for long spells on the stones by the river..."

"Did she know that man who was killed?" I asked in a manner I judged to be the most ingenuous and natural in the world...

"Yes, of course, she saw him every morning..." Don Melchor brightened up as he returned to his tale, "...everybody knows everybody here, you see. Of course, the whole town condemned her afterwards... although by that time she was already gone, leaving some suitors behind because... let me tell you, there in the village, a woman's beauty is prized more than her intellect..."

"Did this woman and this man know each other?" My question bore an emotional charge that I could not hide. "Was there something between them? Were they seen together? Were they... lovers?"

"No, *señor*, they were not lovers..." Don Melchor adopted a grave and morbid tone. "She was his killer."

I didn't hear that. I didn't believe it. I didn't want to believe it. I didn't pay it the slightest attention. I'd suddenly become autistic. It was an absurd suggestion. A falsehood, pure and simple. My mother was highly irritable; she had fits of rage that overwhelmed her completely, but no impulse would have been so powerful to draw her into a spiral of crime. And yet... there was a doubt there, that little sting that pricked my skin and injected it with a worry that contradicted the beliefs that had been sown in my consciousness since childhood. Why did my mother go to such lengths to erase the image of my father from my memory? Why did she bear such a grudge against him that she could not even pronounce his name? Why did she react violently the only time that I ever asked her about him?

"This woman... yes... the one here... she climbed up a ceiba tree along the path to the river just past the fields, and she stayed up there for three days, like an eagle building a nest..." Don Melchor continued to thumb the photos of my mother. "Three days! Nobody realized, but I saw her there because she hadn't come to sleep in my house, where she was staying... yes... she paid me money for rent. When she climbed up the tree she didn't come down to eat, or to sleep, she relieved herself up there too, and I wondered why... until the day came when that man, Emilio was his name, when he passed by there, walking hand in hand with his little boy, and when they went down the path to the river this woman pointed a shotgun at him and blew his head off with a single bullet..."

With his little boy? With no prior warning of its intentions, common sense quietly took up residence in the hole in my gut and, determining that Don Melchor's anecdote was dynamiting the very structure of my being, declared the interview over. I felt the bubbling of an acidic magma that welled up in my stomach, my vision clouded over like a premature symptom of glaucoma and I began to hear a deafening buzzing as if a cicada had nested deep inside my eardrum. Instinctively, I lowered my head until the point of my chin came into contact with my breastbone, breathed heavily while my throat emitted a bellowing sound like a bull in the matador's ring, pulled myself up awkwardly and staggered towards the door that led out to the plot of land... but before reaching the outdoors, a sudden attack of successive retching knocked me to the ground and an disgusting mucous liquid gushed from my mouth, as if my body were warning me of the need to suspend the obsessive exploration into the dark recesses of my past, and to stop wondering who I am, what I am, where I came from and where I'm going with this incomprehensible and excruciating burden of shame, anger, fear and guilt.

2

HER REAL NAME was Sandra Jacobs. Her aliases were Julieta Sanchez (the name I knew her by) and Regina Montero. She had studied Political Sciences in the Department of Political and Social Sciences at the National Autonomous University of Mexico, and had joined the ranks of Research and National Security in the final year of her degree program. She had been an outstanding student. From the moment of her recruitment, she had displayed a particular inclination towards order, neatness, personal grooming and cleanliness. She was extremely disciplined. She had proven herself adept in the use of firearms. She had also demonstrated a facility for animal training, particularly with horses. She'd had, according to a brief psychological profile that I studied in detail, "family problems that left her emotionally disturbed", "a constant tendency to refer to the subject of death in her writings and drawings", and "doubts about her sexual preferences."

In outlining the missions she had carried out, the reports were confused and incomplete, and many of them were incomprehensible. She had been in Guadalajara, Culiacan, and Monterrey, as well as Veracruz, Villahermosa, Campeche, Merida... Tuxtla Gutierrez...

Her telephone in Mexico City had been bugged, because in her biographical record there were several recordings of telephone conversations with various people, from department colleagues to certain family members, including her mother, an uncle, some friends in public office and... Captain Rodolfo Miranda, the man who had followed her to New York and who was evidently also an agent with Research and National Security in the Ministry of Internal Affairs. It appeared, from what I could infer from the correspondence, that this Captain Miranda had been her contact, the agent who had recruited her on the university campus, the person charged with tracking her so as to monitor her and, probably, to restrict her moves and prevent information from filtering to outsiders...

My mother's name was Sandra Jacobs? Her photograph identified her unmistakably. It was years old, of course, but she had the same huge eyes, the same dark, shiny hair, the pursed lips that made her look like she was holding back the force of her words. The report was confidential, precise, and to the point. It left no room for doubt. But it was incomprehensible to me, highly disturbing, impossible to assimilate, and, somehow... repulsive.

I had obtained this confidential report on my mother in 2001, taking advantage of the chaos and confusion that followed the change of government in Mexico after the presidential election that ended seventy years of one-party rule, when the security system began to show its first fissures after having been an impenetrable monolith for decades. An old friend from college had got a job at the Center of Investigation and National Security and did me the discreet favor of looking up my mother in the secret files using the photographs I provided and the name of Julieta Sanchez.

And there I was, with all the information before my eyes, but with a mental block that I could not overcome to process it all. I read Sandra Jacobs and thought of my mother smiling at me when I was seven, combing my hair in front of the mirror... I read that she was adept in the use of firearms and I remembered her painting with watercolors in her studio... is it possible that the same person can lead two completely different lives due to some transcendental rupture in her biography, a fork in the road that sent her in a radically different direction? Or could a single person have two simultaneous personalities and reveal them to people according to the circumstances? Was my mother a secret agent for National Security in Mexico, disguised as a waitress in New York? That possibility made me dizzy... I conjured up images of my mother and I saw a happy woman buying me ice cream or picking me up from school... my mother saving my life in the subway, my mother lending money to the bankrupt neighbors, my mother serving so many people in so many restaurants, my mother smiling at Robert De Niro... and then, taking a revolver from her handbag and shooting somebody with the cold blood of a professional killer who is simply following orders. No, the whole thing was absurd... and yet... there were so many questions that I had never asked myself until that moment. Why had she flown into a rage when I discovered that she jealously guarded all those photographs of Sophia Loren posing sensuously before the camera? Why hadn't she had a single man after my father? How had she managed, without any kind of training, to snatch me from the jaws of death on the subway platform and to save Mrs. Wharton from the fire the day that our apartment building went up in flames? In that moment, plagued by all these uncertainties, I decided that I could not go on without confronting her directly.

So I hid away the copy of the report that my friend had obtained for me, with the due level of caution suitable for such a valuable document. In spite of my blindness, it had opened my eyes. Much was missing, of course. They'd forgotten to include in her logbook that she had been "commissioned to investigate the activities of Emilio Montalvo, subversive agent with Trotskyite affiliations, with whom she ended up having a child... followed him faithfully across the states of Campeche, Yucatan and Quintana

Roo, and when she completed her investigations she ended his life in Tenosique County in Tabasco..." Nor does it mention that "this mission was the last of her life, as afterwards she fled the country with her son, and her whereabouts are now unknown..."

In the end, the document left me with a long list of unanswered questions.

3

I ARRIVED IN Manhattan in September. It was the month of perfect weather in New York; young people dance around the Village on roller-skates with their ghetto blasters blaring, the summer heat begins to dissipate and an atmosphere of calm pervades the city as the leaves start to fall from the elms and the days grow gradually shorter. My work with the World Bank was covering my travel expenses at that time, and for the first time in my life I stayed at the Lexington Hotel. Ironically, at that time I could have given my mother the money that I'd promised her many years before when I'd left my childhood behind me years before.

Although I'd resolved to get to the heart of the truth with my mother, I cannot deny that I was afraid of her reaction. The last time I spoke with her was at our eventful breakfast at the Plaza Hotel, when I'd ended up bathed in honey and fruit like the god Bacchus. After that, I'd had no contact with her again, and she probably had no interest in another meeting. My mother was the haughty type; she was incapable of forgiving a serious offense. But... what was the offense? Showing her a photograph of my father? Only after my conversation with Don Melchor Ortega did I understand the extremeness of her reaction... but I didn't want a repeat performance.

On the second day of my stay I decided to call her on the phone. I waited for the most appropriate time to reach her after work, but when I called I got her answering machine. The first time I left no message. The second time I said I wanted to see her, that I was at the Lexington, room 304, so she could return my call. After a day of waiting, she still hadn't called back.

On the third day, I determined to meet her at work. I headed for the café on 24th Street, near the Chelsea Hotel, and sat down again at the table in front of the big window where Robert De Niro had sat and spoken with her years before... nothing. I waited for her service in vain... I began watching the movements of the staff who came out of the kitchen, the waitresses and the bellhops, until I had convinced myself of her absence. Finally, a waitress confirmed that she no longer worked there.

In that interregnum, I realized that I was on the point of committing the same error I'd made two years earlier, when I showed her my father's photo without warning. She didn't merely dislike such surprises; they threw her off her rails... and I was on the verge of making the same mistake again, because I'd brought with me the confidential report I had from Intelligence and National Security to show her without any prior warning. This would have provoked a reaction similar to the launching of the fruit plate, or something even more radical... better not even to think of it. What occurred to me then was to fill her in a little first, to explain the motive of my visit, to talk to her of the growing collection of doubts that tormented me every day, and of my pressing need for explanations. Only she could clear up all the mysteries. So I decided to send her the full report by email, to give her time to analyze it first... and also to avoid a reaction of fury in my presence, in case she had one, which was highly probable. So I set down to transcribe the report on the computer at the hotel. I sent the whole thing to her email address, and so that she could verify its authenticity I photocopied the document and sent it to her house by courier. Nervously, I awaited her initial response, a telephone

call with her voice wavering, an emotional avalanche of accusa-
tions.... nothing.

The days passed, and I began to consider the possibility of
showing up at her house as if nothing had happened, when a
package arrived at the hotel with my name on the front. At recep-
tion they told me that it hadn't arrived by ordinary courier, but
had been delivered by a messenger, a thin, well-dressed man who
left it on the counter without an explanation... Captain Miranda?
No, he couldn't still be a thin man after so many years. Inside the
envelope was a VHS videotape, and I had to buy a video recorder
to be able to view its contents in my hotel room.

That day, I remember well, my stomach began its long pilgrim-
age down the road towards gastritis.

The video began with the image of an empty room with a
white wall in the background and a single chair in front of it. It
looked like a prison, an interrogation room or a deserted house,
as if the producer of the recording had wanted to give the impression of a neutral and unrecognizable location. After a few seconds,
my mother appeared, her face rigid and her gaze fixed firmly
towards the lens of the camera. I had last seen her some years
before, and for the first time I saw in her face the marks of the relentless passage of time. Her eyes, as large as ever, seemed slightly
duller under the weight of her eyelids; the line of her nose had lost
its fineness, and the dimples that formed when she smiled had
turned into grooves that gave her a more solemn appearance. She
was casually dressed, in one of those grey tailored suits that she
liked so much, but her attitude made her clothing look stiffer.

Everything was arranged to focus the attention of the viewer
on the weight of her words. There was no decorative plant on
screen, nor any painting or adornment, nothing that might have
distracted from the important message that came next. My mother
sat fully erect in the chair and her face wore only the vaguest hint
of a smile. The camera didn't move and there were no close-ups

of any kind, which suggested that my mother had arranged the Spartan cinematography on her own.

"Emilio," she began, the first time as far as I remember that she had ever called me by my name, "I have preferred to speak to you this way because it is less uncomfortable for me to say what I want to say... I know that we have become very distant, not only geographically, but also morally and emotionally. You are now a man, you've had some important achievements, you've continued your studies on your own, and I... I am now an older woman, with the better part of my life behind me. It is natural that, after so many years of living together, we've had differences..." (here there is a cut, suggesting that she hadn't liked what she'd said next and had edited it out) "...and as you are now a fully grown man, of an age to understand everything going on in the world, whether for good or ill, I'm going to talk openly to you about my history, and above all of that part of my history that is also your history... Remember when you asked me to speak to you truthfully when you invited me to breakfast at the Plaza Hotel? Well, now you will have your wish... but... don't worry, I'm not going to talk to you about my whole life, only that part that has interested you so much lately and that has pushed you on a search far and wide... yes, I have here the report about me from the Center of Investigation and National Security... I should tell you that I hadn't seen it before..." (here she laughs sarcastically) "...what did you think about that part where it says that I 'have doubts in relation to my sexual preferences'...?" (she grows serious again) "...well, no, the fact is I don't have doubts... it's simply that I have no sexual preferences..." (she lowers her head with a kind of shame, as if searching for the right words to address the topic, and then she lifts it again haughtily) "...I do not deny that I have liked some men, some women, but I have been devoted to another cause, one far more important. Yes... of course, I have worked for the national security of my country, and in a certain way I still do... nobody can just leave a job like that; it is not a job that you can quit. No, once you take a place in the ranks of Central Intelligence you can never leave them behind... because by working for Mexican Security you receive information that others don't, and this makes you a source of potential information that must be jealously guarded... do you understand? That is why I – as you already know – am so reserved when it comes to my private life... like any other person, come to that, because your private life is just that, a *private* life, and nobody has the right to interfere in it..." (here there is another cut in the filming) "...but as far as my private life affects you, let me tell you that the report you were given is correct, and all the rest as well... I don't regret it... No, I don't regret anything. They trained me, taught me to handle pistols, rifles, machine guns, and I agreed to do it... they gave me classes in counter-insurgence, they taught me about the dangers that existed for Mexico, the proliferation of terrorist groups in different parts of our Republic, and the threat of a violent uprising... and that uprising came, of course. Remember the Zapatistas in 1994? So you see they weren't so far wrong... but in those years, in the decade of the seventies, guerrillas were springing up everywhere, and it was necessary to stop them at all costs... so..." (here the cut includes a longer pause, because my mother appears again with her hair arranged and her lips redder) "...let me tell you what leftists and guerrillas are... You most probably don't know, no, in your childhood in New York nobody ever talked about it, but the guerrilla group is a closed organization, authoritarian, horribly bloody, with an implacable discipline, operating in secret, that takes away the individual liberty of its members and that executes any member who betrays its principles... or any enemy... that's why it's so dangerous. It is not easy to penetrate such a group... nor is it easy to get out of one. Of course, they claim that all their crimes are justified, they speak of the ideals of equality, social justice, the rule of the proletariat, the kingdom of the poor in this world, but at the end of the day, what they want is to impose a dictatorial government without political opposition parties, a pyramid structure with a single man at the top... this is all really before your time, but in every country where guerrilla groups have taken over, despotic and bloody governments have been imposed. There was Stalin in the Soviet Union, Mao-Tse-Tung in China, the Khmer Rouge in Cambodia, Fidel Castro in Cuba.... but... I don't want you to think that I want to get off topic... so returning to the subject of your interest, I had been preparing myself physically and mentally for a long time... when I was in the Department of Political Sciences, I went to classes regularly, but at the same time I was in contact with the people from Security. I received training, I studied the strategies of terrorist groups, we went on field simulations, always with due discretion... shhhh...." (here she raises her index finger to her lips as if calling for silence) "... I didn't know my fellow agents... and so I was working in secret until they assigned me my first mission... and on that mission I went to the southeast of the country. I met your father, a farmer belonging to that sector we call the rural middle class, a hard-working man with initiative, but he had fallen into the hands of the terrorists. They had washed his own ideas out of his head, they had convinced him to join a terrorist cell, they were training him, and because he had charisma, he was potentially very useful to them... a guerrilla leader in the making. And so somebody had to stop all that, to stop his march towards hell. Nobody knew it, no, but those Marxist groups, Leninists, Maoists and Trotskyites, were planning bank robberies, kidnappings of business leaders, attacks on public offices, armed uprisings, mass murders... maybe the name of the business chief from Monterrey, Eugenio Garza Sada, means nothing to you, or the governor of the state of Guerrero, Ruben Figueroa, people who were kidnapped and in some cases killed by guerrilla groups... of course, the lives of these people didn't matter to them; after all, they were enemies, prominent members of the bourgeoisie, exploiters of the working class, public enemies and the other names they labeled them with... someone had to stop them. That's why the government created institutions for the protection of national security... and they started recruiting people. Someone had to act, with conviction and devotion... and that someone was me. That's what they'd trained me for, that's what I was being prepared for all that time..." (here her voice breaks, although her face reflects a coldness that seems positively bulletproof) "...I want to tell you that I don't regret it. I am more convinced every day that I did the right thing. I did it for the good of Mexico, yes, but also for your own good, because you had a father who was a good man, a naïve man... but who had been tricked, manipulated and indoctrinated in such a way that he would have been an appalling example as a father... and now, instead, look at you, take a look at yourself, look what you've made of your life, you are the proof that I was right. You didn't turn into a criminal... and above all..."

I turned off the video player. I didn't want to hear any more of her defense. She was telling me that she, my mother, had killed my father... in the name of Mexico? I had never heard anything so absurd. But what offended me most deeply was not her political speech against terrorism, but the hypocritical argument that what she had done, the most aberrant act in the world, had been for my own good... for my own good? My spirit was broken, but I was still psychologically stable, and this allowed me to leave aside the tangle of contradictory emotions that choked up my insides for a moment and to consider all the despicable nonsense that I had just heard and to process them in the section of my addled brain that was reserved for rational thought. Thus I was able to categorize my mother's discourse into a series of arguments. According to my mother, she had acted rightly, following her perverse logic, because by murdering my father she had liberated me from a paternal example that might have turned me into a criminal, a debauchee, or another member of the guerrilla forces that tormented the world with their threats. Is this a sensible argument? How can a person decide what is good or bad for another person, even if that person is a child? Even if that person is *her* child? What did she think she was doing? Acting in legitimate defense? In defense of her son? No, it was too senseless. And independently of the relationship she had with the victim (hadn't she loved him at some moment? Had she lived with him before his "conversion" to terrorism?) and her relationship with me, what she had done was, quite simply, a crime. To her, she was following orders, she was a cog in the machinery of State Security, but... did that justify murder? The question is not easily answered; there are probably legions of lawyers debating the issue... in the case of a war, for example, the solider who does not obey an order and does not shoot against the enemy is a traitor, and can be judged by a military tribunal... but... was Mexico at war? Of course not... and... beyond all this was the incontrovertible fact, attested to by an eyewitness, that my mother had climbed a tree to hide herself for several days, had waited until my father passed by on the road – *walking hand in hand with his little boy* – and had shot him while he was unarmed and defenseless. Could I go on living with such a weight on my shoulders?

4

AFTERWARDS, I FINISHED watching the video (it didn't offer much more of importance after what I've already described) and I went to bed.

Shortly before dawn that night, I woke up with a headache. I turned on the bedside lamp in my hotel room and lay staring at the ceiling a while. The only thing up there was a fire alarm, that little device that registers smoke and heat in the room and sounds a warning in response. Meanwhile, in my head, the alarm had already gone off. My whole life was in flames. My mother... how was it possible that she had committed such a barbaric act? I had heard of domestic violence before, but... domestic assassinations? Had we returned to the days of Caligula? No, it wasn't possible... was there anyone in the world who had experienced what I was going through? No, nobody. Other people lived normal lives; they had a right to happiness. For the first time in my existence, I felt overwhelmed by pure hatred, which had been gestating over the last months of my investigations. I had no father. I'd had one, but he'd been taken away. This detail, which had hovered in the shadows of my consciousness as the lingering sense of an absence, came back to me now to claim the vengeance that was its due. I was full of rancor, that dark fluid that swells up from the pit of the stomach until it reaches the esophagus, covers the palate and nests in the protuberances of the brain. As a child, there was something that distinguished me from other children; I hadn't known, or even wondered, who my father was. All the other kids had a father. Many of them had an estranged father, living in conjugal exile, but a father all the same; another individual responsible for having brought them into the world. This was not my case, and without knowing it, I had always resented it. Deep down, knowing myself to be different made me feel inferior. And this sense of my own inferiority was compensated for by the grandeur of my mother. She was the strong one, the almighty, the one who could do anything, the smart one, the giver of life, the savior from all dangers. Hadn't she saved my life? Hadn't she saved me from losing a leg to amputation? Ahh, mama, I can't believe what's happened. Tell me it isn't true. Tell me that the farmer in that village in Tabasco lied. Tell me that your work for Mexican Intelligence is an invention. Tell me that you are not the one in that video. Tell me that you are the mother I'd always had, who used to come smiling to me to wake me up. Tell me the truth of life is a lie.

I turned out the light, and tried to sleep again. I couldn't.

5

THAT SAME MORNING at daybreak, I showered quickly, got dressed in a daze and went down into the street. The outlines of the buildings of Manhattan loomed imposingly in the first glimmers of sunlight. I walked down 47th Street to Park Avenue and then headed for the Panam Building and Grand Central Station, which was the only place open at that early hour. I walked in like a zombie through the main entrance and inside I was dazzled by the dimensions of the place: the gigantic mirrors on the walls; the rectangular columns of granite; the magnificent marble stairways. I looked up in awe at that great vault speckled with stars and constellations, and I felt a slight shiver as I contemplated the smallness of humanity against the immenseness of the cosmos.

And humanity was right there to be contemplated, because at that time of early morning there were already dozens of passengers moving around the terminal, coming out of the subway, climbing the ramp to the main concourse, buying newspapers, magazines and cigarettes, sitting in the cafés filling up on the fuel necessary to attack the day, crowding around the information stand and disappearing down the tunnels that led to the platforms.

I climbed the marble stairs towards the balcony level and went on observing the human swarm as it swept from one end of the station to the other... how could I ever again form part of that flow of life after learning my true story? What would I have to do to cast off the role of outsider and reintegrate myself into everyday life? Rising up in front of me like a reminder of my internal exile was the golden arch of the Oyster Bar, the luxury restaurant where my mother had got a job after years of dedication and effort...

I watched the crowd distractedly for a while until just below, at the arrivals and departures information booth, an almost imperceptible movement caught my eye and made me forget my inner turmoil for a moment. In the queue waiting to be attended was a slightly rotund, elderly black man in a very loose-fitting raincoat... and behind him, almost stuck to him, was a short, pale-faced teenage girl who was jerking from side to side as if she wanted to jump the queue and reach the counter first to find out what she needed to know. As they were surrounded by a crowd of people, nobody realized when she slowly slipped her hand into the pocket of the raincoat of the man in front of her and stealthily withdrew a wallet... and then, without anyone noticing, she slipped out of the queue at once and began walking towards 42nd Street with the wallet in her pocket... and then it happened... something inside me, a reaction or a chemical impulse, a sudden glimmer, an irrepressible desire to act, to do something in response to the adversity and injustice in the world... I don't know exactly what it was that moved me to do it, but instinctively I headed for the stairs and went down to the main concourse, intercepting the girl before she made it out to the street...

"Hey," I called to her in the friendliest tone I could manage, "didn't you forget to give back that wallet that you've got in your pocket?"

She looked bewildered and frightened, and beneath her expression was reflected the monster that mercilessly torments every juvenile offender: guilt. At first she tried to run, but I stopped her with a firm grip on her arm.

"If you try to run, I'll call the police," I said in a tone stern and persuasive. "If you give me the wallet, I'll let you go."

The girl made an expression of annoyed resignation, took the wallet out of her pocket, gave it to me reluctantly and then ran for the platforms. I waited until the man had left the information counter to catch up with him and return it to him.

"You dropped this," I said to him quietly.

He examined the wallet, checked that it was not in the pocket of his raincoat, took out the ID cards inside, counted the money in each section, and when he'd verified that nothing was missing he took out a fifty dollar bill and offered it to me as a sign of gratitude or compensation... I didn't accept, in spite of his insistence. I excused myself politely and began to climb the marble stairs again, to return to my lookout and lose myself in my gloomy meditations. And yet, something inside me had changed... a sudden blooming, I don't know... I felt lighter and satisfied, as if acting as I had done had absolved me of all the guilt and angst of my existence... even my surroundings looked different... the sunlight poured in through the large windows and the electric lights inside magnified the space, creating a luminous order in which the arches and the enormous vault, the columns and the walls, the stairs and the ramps all came together in a brilliant universe, in which the latest technology joined forces with a spectacular architecture to carry the citizens of every latitude of the world... that was New York, the melting pot where a universal culture was in gestation and also... my home, at least in that moment.

Then I knew, in that fleeting moment of clarity, what I had to do. The problem was not that I had nowhere to turn. If I was alone, without family, without teachers, without a protector god to guide me, I would take refuge in the only reality that remained among men: the Law.

Why the Law? Man is guided by standards; this is not merely a declaration of the Law and our moral codes, but an easily verifiable truth in everyday life. Rules are not made only for citizens, public servants, police, tax collectors, clergymen, doctors and teachers. Everybody in the world automatically follows their own precepts. Even murderers have their own regulations within the world of crime. Even the insane, those who in a fit of vengeful fury tear off their clothes and run naked through the streets, have limits which are not easily exceeded. Of course, there are visible laws, acknowledged by everyone, but there are also hidden standards that often remain unnoticed by those who follow them blindly. The hermit has an inner law that forbids him to approach others. The terrorist, blinded by his fanaticism, must not acknowledge the humanity of his victims.

All my life, I had blindly followed the standards imposed by my mother. I was an exemplary child; well-behaved, a good student, active, hardworking... and above all, docile. Throughout my childhood, my youth and my coming of age, I had never dared to criticize her. Everything about her seemed to me magnificent, extraordinary and admirable. In my eyes, she was irreproachable. I never doubted her integrity or her competence. I lived by her and for her. I was no more than her appendage.

How would I now dare to denounce her as a murderer? Something imperceptible had happened while I had watched the video, something that had altered the structure of my soul. For the first time, her words had not convinced me. If my father had been a determined guerrilla, a fanatical terrorist, a danger to society, an agent of Stalin or a follower of Fidel Castro, it was not sufficient reason to take his life. It would have been better to have left him, to have denounced him, to have handed him over to justice. But not to rub him out with a bullet to the head. You can't kill someone merely for professing ideas different from your own.

Would it not be inhuman of me to deliver my own mother over to the not always clean hands of justice? What if they condemned her to life in a dark prison cell in Mexico? What if Central Intelligence eliminated her to keep her from saying too much? Could I denounce my mother, who had cared for me with the love of a she-wolf for her cub through the hardest moments of my existence? Was I myself so heartless?

I decided that I would do it. It was the best that I could do to bring some clarity into my miserable existence. I knew, from the bottom of my heart, that to drink from this cup would kill me with its pain.

I felt relieved. I had made the most difficult and heart-rending decision of my life, but it was the only way for me to belong again to humankind, the most diverse, pluralistic, misunderstood, extraordinary and vile species on this planet.

6

I left Grand Central Station and headed for the subway, taking
the green line to City Hall. By mere coincidence, I observed the
opulent court buildings as I passed, the Supreme Court, all the
grand architecture of the judicial framework of the U.S. political
system, that complex that crowns the south of the island around
the city's government. It seemed as if those emblematic buildings
were the backdrop to the decision I'd just made.

In those moments of determination and anxiety, I felt an obvious urgent need to locate my mother. I wanted to bid her farewell in peace, like you would at a funeral. At that point, I didn't
know where she was working. I didn't know where to find her. I
had no leads. While I wandered, I was struck by a providential
idea: to call the Andersons, those neighbors who visited her so
often to exchange hopes and hardships on their free evenings. So
I walked down the street alongside the park near City Hall until I found a phone booth with a not very voluminous but user-
friendly phonebook.

"Mrs. Anderson? This is Emilio..."

Mrs. Anderson, it seemed, had not spoken to anyone on the
phone in a long time. Or perhaps her old age had brought with
it new obsessions, and she had acquired the habit of prolonging

her phone calls beyond the limits of patience. However, the information she provided was decisive. My mother was working a lot, more than she should be in Mrs. Anderson's opinion, but thanks to her perseverance she had climbed to the highest rungs of the social scale of New York restaurants, and had reached the peak; she was no longer a waitress but a hostess...

"...she works now at a restaurant called Windows on the World..."

Booom! A deafening noise hit me right at the base of my cerebellum and the receiver dropped from my hand. I thought it was a traffic accident, a brutal collision on Church Street between two freight trucks, a gas tank explosion or a collapse on a nearby construction site; I could not have imagined the global magnitude of what had just happened. The first thing I saw around me was a monumental confusion, people in the street running in every direction as if seeking refuge, and I ran too without knowing the reason; cars were stopped in the middle of the road as if they'd stalled and on the corner of Broadway and Barclay I noticed that people were looking up and... then I saw that one of the towers of the World Trade Center was in flames.

A fire! All along Barclay Street the people crowded around on the sidewalk wearing expressions of astonishment and fear, paralyzed by the sight of glass raining down from above, mixed with papers, steel fragments, dismembered human body parts, office furniture, shoes, shards of porcelain, the broken remnants of aircraft seats... *it was a plane...* the sirens squealed in every direction, people appeared in the street with their arms or faces scorched, and a smell of singed death filled the air all around...

Horrified, I spun my body around and tried to flee towards Greenwich Street, when a collective howl stopped me and made me turn my eyes back to the sky; then I saw clearly, as if in slow-motion, a second plane fly directly into the other tower with diabolical marksmanship, cutting the air with an apocalyptic explosion, and hurling out a ball of flame in the impact. It was pandemonium. What followed was an unceasing nightmare in which pain, desperation, fear, agony and death all joined forces. As in dreams, I lost all sense of space and time. The street began to fill with burned and bloody bodies while people fell from the sky; people who had hurled themselves from the building to avoid dying in the flames. You only needed to look up to see bodies leaping into nothingness and crashing inert onto the roofs of the neighboring buildings, or onto the asphalt that singed from the closeness of the fire. It was a spectacle of Dantesque and at the same time heroic proportions, because there were also firefighters, police officers and ordinary citizens who were rushing to the aid of the wounded, and struggling with all their might to save the lives of anyone they could. Many tore off their clothing to offer a bandage to one of the injured. This exemplary response kept me from joining the stampede of those who fled. In the chaos I found a school full of children, where women were crowding around trying to get their sons and daughters out, and without thinking I pushed my way in to help with the evacuation of the smallest. They were children of three, four, five years of age, who came out crying in anguish and panic, and I carried them through the smoke and out to the street and passed them to any person who offered a hand. In their desperation, many mothers were squashing the little kids in the way, while others fell victim to attacks of hysteria or fainting... I don't know how much time I spent in the inferno. In the street, there was a car that had the radio on at full volume, and in the distance I could hear that the city was paralyzed, the bridges had been closed, the Empire State Building and the U.N. building had been evacuated, the airport had closed its doors and the skies were under military patrol. Then, one of the towers collapsed, throwing up a cloud of smoke, dust, dirt, glass and debris that spread out quickly through the streets all around it. I saw the cloud move in menacingly, and a man with panic drawn on his face came running towards me. I turned around and ran as fast as my legs would allow, breathing the dense and burning air... I ran like a madman, ready for anything, to jump into the Hudson or climb the highest fence, to step over anyone who got in my way. I panted in anguished horror as I tried to suck in air by the mouthful... I ran like this for several blocks until my lungs failed me... my legs could have gone on running, but the thick dust storm made breathing impossible, and I had to stop, a savage cough forcing me to improvise a handkerchief before I could go on... the atmosphere was a chalky cloud that spread out over southern Manhattan and the people around me were an army of zombies bathed in ash and blood, surrounded by the incessant ululation of the police and ambulance sirens, and with expressions lost in the horizon of devastation and death...

Walking among the spectral faces and the avenues in ruins, I have no idea how I got to the evergreen riverfront of Battery Park. Behind me was the island covered in an ominous cloud of smoke and mourning... and ahead, with the undaunted glory of better days, the Statue of Liberty raised her torch indifferently, as if liberty and death were the two inseparable faces of life itself...

The last thing I remember is falling onto the grass and adding my voice to a collective wail of mourning, like a soldier collapsing from exhaustion and misery after a defeat...

7

Was there some connection between the terrorist attack and my decision to deliver my mother over to justice? None in the least. The question itself was utterly senseless. The slightest suggestion of an association of this kind would be a symptom of an obvious case of schizophrenia or mental decay. But deep down inside me, there was an alarm that went off whenever I overstepped the limits set by my mother, and even on this occasion I could not escape from this fatal mechanism by way of reasoning, however convincing that reasoning might be. Since my childhood, my mind had connected the many rages of my mother with natural catastrophes, gale force winds, tornadoes and earthquakes. The slightest annoyance could have unleashed chaos. I had inside me an elaborate tripwire that ensured obedience, an explosive cartridge that would blow up at the slightest provocation, loaded with overwhelming doses of fear, punishment, suffering and guilt.

Still, I wanted to see her. Before bringing her before justice, I wanted to say goodbye. Perhaps, I needed to forgive her. The Law would not. But I needed to cleanse myself, to unload all my resentment. So I went to look for her at her house. On September thirteenth, I crossed the Brooklyn Bridge, just like I used to, and sat myself down in front of her house. The front porch was shut and the daily newspaper was up against the door, but the house did not give the impression of being long abandoned. Somebody lived there, although at that moment that somebody was not inside. What should I do? Wait for her arrival at dusk? Come back the next day?

I called the Andersons.

Claire Anderson answered again. The moment she heard my voice, she began crying inconsolably. She repeated the name of the restaurant where my mother was working as hostess, the pinnacle she'd reached after a career full of hard work and sacrifice.

"It was Windows on the World, oh dear…"

Until that day, I had not been aware of the address of the restaurant. It was in the North Tower of the World Trade Center, on the 107th floor.

EPILOGUE

1

My mother was not Sandra Jacobs.

This devastating revelation reached me through the cybernetic magic of email. From an address impossible to trace, as is all related to Mexico's National Security, Captain Rodolfo Miranda sent me a concise communiqué. It was dated April 4, 2002.

It read as follows:

Dear Mr. Emilio Montalvo Sanchez,

I have learned through various sources that you have been seeking information about your deceased family members for some time. Out of respect for the relationship that you and I shared for several years, although it was always distant and neutral, I feel an obligation to offer you some information that may be of interest to you.

Firstly, I wish you to know that Ms. Sandra Jacobs, alias Julieta Sanchez – as you knew her – was not your biological mother. Your biological mother was Mrs. Margarita Sanchez, the wife of Mr. Emilio Montalvo Galvez, with whom she had two sons. Both sons have the same name, as when she lost the first – which was you – she gave the same name to the second, with whom she was pregnant at the time.

As you know, Sandra Jacobs, killed in the terrorist attack of September 11, 2001 in New York City, was a secret agent for the Mexican federal government, and was the person who ended the life of your father. At that time, you were two years and a few months old, and were accompanying your father along the path on which he died. After eliminating him, Agent Sandra Jacobs took you into her custody, due to your being orphaned by the accomplishment of her mission, and she requested permission to leave the country with you. The rest of the story you already know.

Margarita Sanchez is unaware that you are still alive.

I recommend that you erase this message. If you make mention of it to anybody else, or use it for any purpose, I will deny its authorship, and you will get yourself into trouble.

Yours sincerely,

Captain Rodolfo Miranda

2

A CEREBRAL EMBOLISM occurs when an artery carrying the blood flow to the back of the head is obstructed by a coagulation of blood and the oxygen supply to the brain is thus suspended; without oxygen, cerebral tissue dies within minutes. As a result, the parts of the body under the control of those tissue cells cease to function properly.

My mother had arterial hypertension, but was not in the habit of checking her pressure frequently. As she was a very hard-working woman, she had no time to see doctors or go to health clinics. Several years earlier, she had migrated with her sister Matilde from Escárcega to Campeche, and together they set up an economical little restaurant specializing in seafood. After a while, their clientele began to grow, the business prospered and doubled in size, and my mother came to enjoy an income unthinkable for a widow without an education or resources and more familiar with the raising of chickens and pigs. She worked from sunrise to sunset in the kitchen and the administration of the business, until one dark day when one of those blood clots clouded her vision and she was taken to hospital. There, her condition stabilized and she was put on occupational therapy and speech therapy, which lifted her spirits in the first few months but did not produce any long-term improvement in her condition. In her last weeks, her organism displayed the characteristic symptoms of deterioration: it became increasingly difficult for her to cook or to bathe, to keep her balance when she walked or sat, or to remain standing long before fatigue overwhelmed her. And more recently, her memory and speech problems had come back.

"Mama, this is Emilio," my brother said to her, after warning me of the dangers of provoking strong emotions in her, "he has the same name as me, you see... I met him over in Paris..."

My mother lay in an old-fashioned iron bed with bars at the head, and with a mattress that was higher than the nightstand, on which sat a lamp and her medication. She was in the bedroom of her house, a French-style construction with only one floor, typical of the houses in Campeche's city center. She had been sleeping when we entered her room, and in the first moments of silence I'd had time to look over her face; she was a mature woman, not much more than fifty years of age, with graying hair and a countenance that was prematurely aged by work and illness; she was a *mestiza*, a woman of mixed blood, with large eyes and a nose turned up like a slide; her mouth was small and a birthmark next to her lip gave her a vaguely coquettish look. How would this face have looked thirty-five years earlier, when she brought me into the world?

"Blujjj em reet," she said with some effort.

When she opened her eyes, my mother stared at me with an expression that I interpreted as mild surprise. Then she turned towards my brother with a neutral and peaceful look, and finally looked around for her sister, who was by her side next to the bed. Then she returned her gaze to Emilio, as if just recognizing him, and began to laugh out loud. She opened her arms in a sign of joy, ready for a hug, and said:

"You brought me fish?"

"Of course, *mamá linda*," Emilio gave me a wink, appealing for my understanding, "I brought you everything you asked me for..."

After Emilio greeted her effusively, I moved closer to the bed-side. I leaned over her, and noticed that she opened her eyes as wide as she could. I smiled. Slowly, I took a small gift out of a bag. It was a sphere a little larger than a baseball, with the figure of the Statue of Liberty inside, and a simulated snowfall. I brought the sphere up to my mother's eyes, turned it upside down and then upright again to demonstrate the climatic effects of the souvenir. I said to her:

"I come from New York, *señora*... I brought you this gift..."

She took it delicately, examined it a moment and then took me by the hand. Then she pulled me towards her weary eyes to see my face up close. She looked at me with a very deep look, smiled lightly and placed the palm of her free hand upon my cheek...

When I walked out of her house, I breathed deeply, and caught a whiff of the sea in the air. A monastic sense of peace invaded my senses completely. It was the sensation of a stage of my life com-pleted, like the feeling that besieges sailors when they return to port. The sensation was not strange to me; I had felt it before, but not as intensely as on this occasion. For the first time in my life, as if I had just been born, I entered fully into the kingdom of this world.

ABOUT THE AUTHOR

MARIO HUACUJA IS a Mexican writer with four previous published novels to his credit: *Temblores,* about the war that rocked Central America in the seventies and eighties; *Las Dos Orillas del Río,* tracing the historical divide that separates the U.S. and Mexico; *La Resurección De La Santa María,* based on the sea voyage the author himself took in an old caravel from Acapulco to Japan, and *El Viaje Más Largo,* a fictional account of Magellan's first voyage around the world. Huacuja has also worked as a university professor, television and radio script writer, and a communications expert in various government departments. *In the Name of the Son* is the first of his novels to be translated into English.